Praise for

YOU ASKED FOR PERFECT

"Wise, romantic, and painfully relatable. *You Asked for Perfect* and Laura Silverman delivered."

—Becky Albertalli, award-winning author
of *Simon vs. the Homo Sapiens Agenda*

"Never before have I read a book that so perfectly captures the stress of being a high-functioning student, the feeling of being caught between crushing expectation and cold reality, and the fear that we'll never be able to do enough. But what makes this story really special is its lasting message of forgiveness—both of others and of ourselves. This was something I desperately needed in high school, and I am beyond joyed that students of any age have it now."

—Francesca Zappia, author of *Made You Up*

"*You Asked for Perfect* is…perfect. Silverman's novel hit me straight in the heart. It made me think about the ways I ask too much of myself and others, and it was powerful enough to make me want to be a better—yet still imperfect—person."

—Bill Konigsberg, award-winning author of *Openly Straight* and *The Music of What Happens*

"An ode to overachievers. Laura Silverman's novel brims with authenticity, from the descriptions of Ariel's Jewish family to the agony that comes with failing a calculus quiz. This is a book for anyone who's ever struggled with the high expectations we set for ourselves."

—Rachel Lynn Solomon, author of *You'll Miss Me When I'm Gone* and *Our Year of Maybe*

"Silverman writes a coming-of-age novel that will charm readers with its relatable and diverse characters, quirky storyline, and interweaving of faith, queerness, and the everyday lives of seniors navigating the pressures of college applications, grades, and relationships. Heartwarming and engaging."

—*Kirkus Reviews*

Praise for Laura Silverman's

GIRL OUT OF WATER

"*Girl Out of Water* swept me up in its wake and did a perfect kickflip on my heart. With a cast of characters worthy of every reader's love, Silverman explores the confusing depths of the teenage experience, and its ebbs and flows, with humor, grace, and savvy."

—John Corey Whaley, Printz winner and author of *Where Things Come Back*

YOU ASKED
FOR PERFECT

ALSO BY LAURA SILVERMAN

Girl Out of Water

YOU
ASKED
FOR
PERFECT

LAURA SILVERMAN

sourcebooks
fire

Published by Sourcebooks Fire, an imprint of Sourcebooks, Inc.
P.O. Box 4410, Naperville, Illinois 60567-4410
(630) 961-3900
Fax: (630) 961-2168
sourcebooks.com

Library of Congress Cataloging-in-Publication Data

Names: Silverman, Laura, author.
Title: You asked for perfect / Laura Silverman.
Description: Naperville, Illinois : Sourcebooks Fire, [2019] | Summary: Ariel
Stone is the perfect college applicant until a failed Calculus quiz sends his
grades into a tailspin that can only be halted by a handsome tutor, but adding a
burgeoning romance to his other commitments may push Ariel past his limit.
Identifiers: LCCN 2018041050
Subjects: | CYAC: Academic achievement--Fiction. | Perfectionism (Personality
trait)--Fiction. | Dating (Social customs)--Fiction. | Homosexuality--Fiction. |
High schools--Fiction. | Schools--Fiction. | Jews--United States--Fiction. |
Muslims--United States--Fiction.
Classification: LCC PZ7.1.S543 Yo 2019 | DDC [Fic]--dc23
LC record available at https://lccn.loc.gov/2018041050

Printed and bound in the United States of America.
VP 10 9 8 7 6 5 4 3 2 1

For Raya Siddiqi—
You brightened up my life.
Rest easy, sweet girl.

YOU ASKED FOR PERFECT

ONE

My feet pound the ground, and sweat drips down my face. With four miles down and one to go, I ease my pace to a comfortable jog and switch from my *Crime and Punishment* audiobook to The Who. All around me, the neighborhood yawns awake, people walking dogs and piling their kids into cars. The sun, which was creeping out of darkness when I left home, now lounges low in the sky.

Finally, I make it back to my driveway. Breathing hard, I massage a stitch in my side and check my phone to find I ran a minute faster than average. Nice. I crack my neck, then head into the house. Mom left early this morning. She's a journalist for the *Atlanta Standard* and was muttering something about a two-faced politician as she rushed to get ready. And my sister is already at elementary school, so Dad and I are the only ones home.

I find him futzing around in the kitchen, already dressed for work in gray slacks and a lavender button-up. "Morning, Ariel!" He spins to face me. His hair, dark and curly like mine, probably should've been cut weeks ago. "Eggs? Oatmeal? Smoothie?"

"Smoothie would be awesome," I say. "Shower. Be back down in a minute."

"You can take five minutes if you want!" he shouts after me as I climb the stairs two at a time. In my bathroom, I strip then step into the shower. Icy water blasts me before it has a chance to warm, and my muscles protest the cold. "Crap, stretches," I mutter.

I press both palms against the shower wall and stagger my legs, bending my right knee and extending my left calf. As the water warms up and cascades over me, I bow my head, taking a few long breaths and stilling for a moment. But then it's time to switch legs, then time for my quads. I wash quickly after.

A few minutes later, I'm back in the kitchen, a bit uncomfortable in damp jeans and holding my Fleetwood Mac T-shirt so it doesn't also get wet.

"New look for school?" Dad asks, sliding a berry smoothie across the counter. He's drinking a kale one. Nasty.

"Yeah, all the cool kids are going shirtless these days." I climb onto the stool at the breakfast bar. My calculus textbook is on the counter, notebook wedged between the pages. I open it with one hand while checking my phone with the other. Water from my damp hair drips down my neck as I read a message from Sook, my best friend.

Running five minutes late

I text back: *No problem*

And it isn't a problem. She's always late. I'd only be screwed if she got here on time. I copy a problem down in my notebook. Usually I do well in math, but there's a long summer between Calculus AB and BC, so it's hard remembering old material.

"Any plans for the weekend?" Dad asks.

I register the question in the back of my head as I stare at my notebook. "Um, usual, I guess."

"We have synagogue tomorrow. And your sister's soccer game is Sunday. Should we make signs since it's the first game of the year? Embarrass her a bit?"

My pencil inches down the page. Crap. What's the next step again? There's a quiz today. I thought I had this down last night. I glance back at the book, while grabbing my graphing calculator. I already did—

"Ariel, signs? What do you think?"

"Huh?"

Dad stares at me like I came from an alien planet and not his own sperm. "You know," he says, "I read an article that said too much studying is detrimental to learning."

"I don't study too much," I reply. "Besides, you were the one up at midnight working last night."

"Yes, but *I'm* an adult, and my brain is already developed. Can I at least help you out with anything?"

"I'm good, Dad."

Workaholics shouldn't try to convince other people to work less. Dad is a civil rights attorney, and he's been known to disappear until three in the morning to work on a case.

If he can stay up late, so can I. Besides, it's just sleep. It's not like I'm taking pills to stay up like some kids at school. That stuff is dangerous.

"Drink your smoothie," Dad says.

"I am." I glance at the glass. It's full.

Dad raises an eyebrow.

I take a sip as my phone buzzes. An email from my safety school. Seems like a mass email, but better safe than sorry. I save it to my college applications folder, then tap my calendar to stare at the only date that really matters. November 1, less than two months from now, when my Harvard application is due.

My phone buzzes again.

Sook: *I'm here*

I slap my textbook closed and shove everything into my bag. "See you tonight," I tell Dad, sliding off the stool.

"Ariel, smoothie. Please?"

Crap. Forgot. My stomach growls. I pick up the cup, push the straw aside, and chug the whole thing. "Ugh." I squeeze my eyes shut. "Brain freeze."

I'm heading out the front door when Dad's voice calls out again. "*Ariel*. Shirt!"

I glance down at my bare chest. Oops.

"Coffee?" Sook asks, passing me a cup of Dunkin' Donuts.

"You are"—I crack a giant yawn—"*the best*."

"This is true." She grins at me.

My best friend is beautiful, warm eyes and smooth skin. She's chubby, her soft white shirt hugging her stomach, and her nails are coated in pink polish. She flips her hair over her shoulder and puts the car into drive.

I groan in comfort as I sink down into her leather bucket seats. Sook's car costs more than the ones my parents drive combined, and I'm not complaining. She drives me to school every morning since there aren't enough parking spots for all the students. I open CalcU, an app with practice problems and tutorials. My eyes run over the formulas.

"Test today?" Sook asks.

"Nah, calc quiz," I say. "What about you?"

"I don't think so?" She shrugs. "I left my planner at school, so I might be forgetting something."

Sook and I have been best friends since sixth grade, when we were placed on the same advanced math track. Back then, she went by her full Korean name, Eun-Sook.

We were "precocious little kids" according to my dad ("bratty little shits" if you ask Sook). We bonded over our mutual drive to be the smartest kids in the class, but these days Sook cares more about her band, Dizzy Daisies, than her grades.

"Oh my god," Sook says, turning up the volume. "You've got to listen to this song."

A gentle acoustic intro builds up to a harder, defiant sound as the drums enter. I nod along. "Pretty good."

"Pretty good? Try incredible. The band is called Carousels, and their lead singer Clarissa is a genius. And also basically the hottest person. Like, absurdly hot. I want to be her, *and* I want to be with her."

I laugh. "Good luck with that. Where does she live? How *old* is she?"

"She's a freshman at the University of Georgia, so only a couple of hours away. Hey, you never know." She turns up the volume more. "God, her voice is everything."

"It is," I agree. Clarissa's voice is grit and fluidity all at once. I glance back at the CalcU app and pick a walk-through problem.

"Maybe we could road-trip to Athens, go see one of her shows," Sook says.

I narrow my eyes. But wait, why would the equation…

"What do you think?" Sook asks.

"Yeah," I say, eyes on my phone. "Maybe."

Ten minutes later, I'm walking into class.

"Morning, Ariel," Pari says, as I slide into my seat in the back row. She spins in her desk to talk to me, eyes bright. Her dark hair is pulled back in a ponytail, and she's wearing leggings and an orchestra T-shirt.

Pari Shah is my sworn enemy. Okay, not really. We're actually friends. But for years we've been competing for both first chair violin and the valedictorian spot. I won the chair, and it looks like I'll also be valedictorian.

At Etta Fields High School, becoming valedictorian is more complicated than perfect grades. We have weighted GPAs, so we earn extra points for AP courses, a 5.0 instead of a 4.0 for an A. The path to the top depends not only on the grades but also on signing up for the right classes.

I edged out ahead of Pari last year when I discovered I could sign up for online AP computer science. It was a monster of a class, but because my high school counts online course grades into our GPAs, it gave me the extra weight to outstrip Pari. I didn't tell her about the class until the registration deadline passed. Vicious. But I'm sure she would've done the same. We both knew one of us would have to win eventually. I'm not going to apologize for being the one to come out on top.

"How's it going?" she asks.

I nod. "Pretty good. You?"

"Good! Well, mostly. I forgot about the quiz until this morning." She laughs. "I guess I have senioritis after all."

"Hah, yeah," I say. "It gets to all of us."

But I eye her with skepticism. There's this thing some AP kids do. We act like we don't care, like those perfect grades appear without effort. We pretend to study only in the five minutes before class, and we shrug our shoulders when teachers hand back tests with As scrawled across the top.

But we also make sure to keep those tests flipped up on our desks, so everyone can see how smart we are and just how naturally it comes.

In a way, it started in truth. I used to get good grades with minimal effort. And I bought into the hype, thought I was awesome. But then the AP classes stacked up. And as the work pressed down on me, I saw through my own bullshit. No one just gets As in all their classes. It's a lie we were telling each other and ourselves.

Pari sneezes, a tiny sneeze. It's kind of cute. I've always thought she was attractive: petite with warm brown skin and quick with a sly comment. But even though I'm attracted to guys and girls, I could never date Pari. She's too similar to me. Too competitive. Too calculating. And I have zero interest in dating myself.

"Gesundheit," I say.

She smiles. "Thanks."

The bell rings. Our teacher Mr. Eller enters the room. Amir

Naeem walks in right behind him. Our eyes connect for a second as he heads to the back row and slides into the desk next to mine. I was surprised he picked this spot on the first day of class, but it is the closest to the window.

I've known Amir forever. Our little sisters are best friends, so I've spent countless family dinners and holidays with him, but we've never clicked. When our families are together, he sits in silence, scrolling on his phone. And he carries his camera everywhere, like the world will end if he doesn't capture a shot of a scavenging bird in the courtyard. Also he only dates older guys. He probably thinks the ones in our grade aren't cool enough for him.

It's just hard to relate to someone who works so hard to be unrelatable.

My gaze flicks over his fitted jeans and plain white V-neck before focusing on my desk. It hasn't escaped my notice that his once-gawky body has filled out with lean muscles.

I shake my head as the second bell rings. "Okay, everyone!" Mr. Eller calls for our attention. "Phones and books away. Hope you studied!"

Quizzes pass down the aisles. One lands on my desk. "Twenty minutes," Mr. Eller says.

I scan the page. Only ten problems. My shoulders tense. When it comes to keeping a perfect GPA, less isn't more. Ten problems mean I can only get one wrong if I want an A.

I want an A.

My pencil wavers above the paper. I take a tight breath and glance around the room. Heads are bent, hands writing.

It's only a quiz...

How much are quizzes worth in this class? I close my eyes and try to visualize the syllabus. Ten percent? Fifteen? I can't remember. Someone coughs in the front of the room.

Okay, I studied. It's fine.

I start working on the first problem, hesitating a bit at each step, double-checking every number. I'm forgetting something. Am I forgetting something? I rub my eyes. I should've slept more.

Pari leans back in her chair. My heart skips a beat. For a moment, I think she's already finished, but she's just stretching.

My pulse thuds in my ears. Light yet piercing like the Mozart piece we're playing in orchestra. All around me, everyone scribbles on the page. Pari stretches again. In the seat next to her, her boyfriend, Isaac, flexes the stress ball he always has out during tests. Amir yawns and scratches his dark stubble.

I can do this. I *have* to do this.

I crack my knuckles. I crack my neck.

Then I bring my pencil back to the page and pick up the pace. With each answer, I gain confidence. It was beginning-of-semester nerves, nothing more. I've got this. I've always got this.

I finish the quiz with time to spare, then lean back and exhale. My right hand shakes lightly. I breathe again. *Relax.* Less than a year to go. Almost there.

Mr. Eller calls, "Time. Pencils down." I go to pass up my paper, but he turns on an ancient projector. "Switch quizzes with the person next to you."

Next to me. The two girls on my right switch papers, which means I'm left with Amir. Of course I am.

"Ariel?" My name is smooth between his lips. The proper pronunciation with the hard *Ar*. Not like *The Little Mermaid*.

My foot shakes as we switch papers. I look down at his quiz. He uses a pen in math class. The confidence irritates me.

Mr. Eller slides the transparency sheet onto the projector. But the answers don't look familiar. Is it the wrong slide?

Wait, no. I stare at Amir's quiz. Every answer matches his neat handwriting.

His answers are right. But I don't recognize most of the numbers. My pen slips in my damp hand. If his answers are right, and my answers don't match his…

Amir looks up at me with an unreadable expression. Oh.

"Trade papers back when you're ready," Mr. Eller says. "We'll go over any questions you have so you're prepared for the test next week."

Without looking at him, I shove Amir's paper in his direction, then hold my hand there, waiting for mine. When I get my quiz back, I can't help but look at the score. Only five out of ten correct. That math I can do. Fifty percent.

I failed.

I am failing calculus.

Dunkin' Donuts coffee swirls like acid in my stomach.

I can feel Amir looking at me. But if I look back, this grade becomes real. And it can't be real because I can't fail calculus. I can't even get a C in calculus because I'll lose the valedictorian spot. And worse, if Harvard defers my decision and puts my application in the regular admission pool, they'll see my fall semester transcript. They'll see a bad grade, my dropped GPA, and they'll reject me.

The bell rings. Everyone stands and collects their things.

"How'd you do?" Pari asks, turning toward me.

I swallow hard. If she finds out I failed, she'll know she has a chance again at valedictorian. She'll bear down, steal my spot. I've got to keep this quiet.

"Yeah, how'd you do?" Isaac asks. He's wearing his football jersey for the game tonight. His white skin is tanned from summer practice.

Amir sits at his desk, messing around on his phone, but I can feel him listening. "I did well," I lie. "Only missed one. Wasn't paying much attention. You guys?"

Isaac shrugs. "Nice. Missed two, but I guess I'll take it."

"One hundred percent," Pari says.

"Of course." Isaac rolls his eyes. "Perfect Pari."

She lightly punches him in the arm. "Shut up."

Isaac winks at her, then turns back to me. "Coming, Ariel?"

"You guys go ahead," I say.

They both leave, and then it's only Amir and me.

He gathers his things and heads down the aisle. I shuffle behind him, keeping his pace with a few feet of distance. I wait until he turns out of the classroom before dropping off my quiz. Then I speed walk out to the hall in case Mr. Eller sees my grade and asks me to stay after class.

In the hallway, heart pounding, I look left and right, before spotting a glimpse of his medium-brown skin. Amir turns the corner, and I chase after him. I've got to ask him to keep this to himself, but if I do it in public, that kind of defeats the purpose. When I'm only steps behind him, I whisper-shout, "Amir!"

He turns, and I point to an empty classroom. "In here," I say. He raises an eyebrow, and the word "please" escapes my mouth.

No one seems to notice as we slip into the room. I shut the door behind us. For a moment, I'm overwhelmed by his scent. Spearmint and basil. I take a short breath, pulse jumping.

"Ariel?" he asks. "Why are we in an empty classroom?"

"That's a very good question," I say.

With the lights off and blinds closed, I'm grateful it's too dim to read his expression. I'm not sure which would hurt more, a look of annoyance or amusement. Not that I care what he thinks of me.

"Ariel?"

"I failed the quiz," I blurt out.

"I know." He shifts. "Is that it?"

"Please don't tell anyone."

"Why would I tell anyone?"

"I don't know." I tug at my pockets. "So you won't? Say anything?"

"No." The warning bell rings. "I'm going to go now...that okay?"

I clear my throat. "Yeah. Fine. I mean, sure. Thanks."

Since when do I get tongue-tied around anyone? I guess since when I fail quizzes. I step to the side, and Amir moves past me and opens the door.

Then he's gone.

I close the door again just so I can bang my head against it.

TWO

"Ariel, do we have an appointment?"

Ms. Hayes, my guidance counselor, looks up from her desk. I'm standing in the doorway of her office, one backpack strap looped over my shoulder. Guidance is busy since it's still the start of the semester, but I don't have the luxury of making an appointment during a lunch period because I don't have a lunch period because I had to make room for an extra AP course. Hopefully Ms. Hayes can squeeze me in before my next class starts.

"Um, no," I say. "Do you have time?"

Her desk is a mess of papers. And there are not one, not two, but three coffee cups in front of her.

"Time, time…" she mutters, clicking her mouse and scanning her computer. "I have exactly five minutes until my next appointment. What's going on?"

Great. Five minutes. That's plenty of time to discuss my entire academic future. I like Ms. Hayes, but she has something like three hundred students assigned to her, so I've been trying to steal spare seconds of her time since freshman year.

"Um." I stand by the chair at her desk, hands gripping the back, as pressure mounts behind my eyes.

Why do I feel like I'm in trouble?

Ms. Hayes picks up her phone and begins typing. Crap. I'm losing her. I need to talk, now. "I failed a math quiz this morning."

Ms. Hayes looks surprised. My stomach constricts. "I'm sorry to hear that. What happened?" She nods to the chairs in front of her. "Go on, sit."

One chair has a towering stack of folders and pamphlets on it, the other a filing box. I move the box to the ground and sit.

"I studied," I say. She peers at me, silent. "I mean, I guess I could've studied more. And my dad kept distracting me this morning. But I thought I had the material down. I mean, it'll be okay, right? It's only one quiz."

"Well, it is only one quiz," Ms. Hayes says. "We can't worry ourselves silly over every little grade."

I breathe out, relaxing a bit.

"But," she continues, "assuming you still want to be valedictorian, it does mean more for you than others. And when a student is taking almost all AP classes, colleges want to make sure they haven't bitten off too much. So, we definitely want to get you back on the right track." She smiles at me. A smile. At a time like this. "Now who teaches AB?"

"It's BC. Mr. Eller."

"Right, of course. Let me see if I can pull up his syllabus." She unwraps a granola bar and bites into it. Then, chewing while clicking around the computer, she says, "Here we go. Okay, quizzes are weighted quite heavily. Twenty-five percent of the grade. Let me check..." She clicks a few more times. "Looks like you have five quizzes this semester, at five percent each, so as you can see... What exactly did you score?"

"Fifty percent," I mutter.

Her silence is punishing. She taps on her phone. "Fifty percent on five percent of your grade, so that's two point five percentage points gone. That's not catastrophic by any standard."

I swallow. "It's not?"

"Not at all. You're still at 97.5 percent. Though the quiz affects your margin of error going forward, which could be challenging as the difficulty of the class increases." She puts down her phone and looks up at me. "Math is an uphill battle."

I pick at the fabric of the seat. "So what do I do?"

Ms. Hayes glances at the clock. "My appointment is running late." She gives a soft smile. "Good news for you. Give me a second. We'll come up with a plan."

I wouldn't be this close to the finish line without Ms. Hayes. Over the years, even in our truncated time together, she put me on the right track, signed me up for the classes I need. She advised me how to audit courses like orchestra so they don't bring down my GPA, how to skip lunch and sign up for zero period classes and take PE online so I could squeeze in extra weighted credits like AP Latin and AP European History.

But I was supposed to be done with all that. I did all the planning, all the maneuvering. The only task left is easy: Get straight As.

And yet I've already messed that up.

"All right." Ms. Hayes rubs her hands together. "First off, have you spoken to Mr. Eller?"

"Not yet."

"Well, I'm sure you know the drill. Ask if you can come in and correct your wrong answers for partial credit. And ask if there's any extra credit work. A few points would make up the grade."

"Right," I say, leaning back. A plan. Some of the tension eases from my muscles. "I should've thought of that. Thank you."

"Second, remember this isn't an excuse to throw all your focus into math and slip up in your other classes. We don't want this creating a domino effect."

"Mm-hmm." I nod and start typing notes into my phone. This is good. I can come back from this.

"Third, it looks like there's a test next Friday, and since studying independently isn't doing the trick, you should get a tutor."

I pause and glance up. "Um…what?"

She sighs. "What is it with kids at this school? Sometimes even the smartest student needs a tutor. That means you."

I shift in my seat. If I get a tutor at school, people will know I'm struggling. Pari has let her guard down. If it stays that way, maybe I could still secure valedictorian with a B in calculus.

"Ariel, what is it?"

"Nothing," I say.

"Look, there are lots of options. You can get a tutor outside of school if you prefer."

There's a knock on the door. A small girl with blond hair stands there. "I'll grab you from the waiting room in a minute, Becca," Ms. Hayes says. The girl nods and leaves. "That's my next appointment. Are you okay for now? You have the steps: go to Mr. Eller, don't forget your other classes, and get a tutor. That's all doable, right?"

"Yup, all doable," I say, my throat tight.

"Excellent." Ms. Hayes smiles. "Make me proud."

A familiar cacophony erupts around me as I open the double doors to the orchestra room. Sliding seats and rockstops squeak across the floor. Lockers slam, metronomes tock, and bows whistle across strings. And over it all, shouts and laughter as people discuss their upcoming weekends.

I spin the combination on my locker and take out my violin case. Every day I bring my violin to and from school so I can practice at home. Last night it sat by the front door because I was too busy with other work. My reading for Spanish Lit is getting ridiculous. It turns out, reading a book in a foreign language takes a *long* time.

I'll have to catch up on practice this weekend. Orchestra should be my easiest class. I'm auditing it, so there's not even a grade. But first chair means all ears are on me, no room for error.

I slip out my phone and check my email. One notification from a safety school and one from Harvard. My heart jumps. I open the email and scan it. *Remember to schedule your alumni interview by...*

I've already scheduled mine. One month from now I'm meeting with Hannah Shultz, CEO of AquaShroom, a hydroponic mushroom company with a fervent user base. I can't help but wonder if the majority of her customers grow a mushroom she can't advertise on her website. I've already prepared study flashcards about Hannah, her company, Harvard history, and my own biography because you can't know your best self too well for any Ivy League interview.

I save the email anyway. I can always confirm with Hannah. Doesn't hurt to be safe.

Pari is at our seats. Is there any way she found out about my grade? No, I'm being paranoid. It's Pari, my friend. Not a secret student spy.

She's running through warm-up scales with diligence. She has tennis practice right after school, so she already changed into a tennis skirt and racer back. I used to rush to soccer practice after the final bell, but I had to leave the team last year. Practice took up too much time, and it's not like being on JV is an impressive enough addition to my college application.

Now, I run on my own. I enjoy it, and occasionally, I'll enter a 10k in attempt to still look like a well-rounded student.

"Hey." I slide into my seat.

"Hey!" Pari responds. "Looking forward to the weekend? Doing anything fun?"

"Think it'll be low-key," I say. "My sister has a soccer game. Gotta cheer her on."

Pari grins. "Y'all are cute. Makes me want an older brother."

"What about you?" I ask. "What are you up to?"

I start tuning my violin, pulling the bow across the string and adjusting the metal screws. I like this part of class. The jumble of notes. Hands warming up. The violin comfortable in my grip.

"Isaac and I are driving up to Nashville tomorrow morning. Gonna check out a museum, go to a concert, and of course, eat delicious barbecue. Don't tell my mother."

I laugh. "Wouldn't dare." Pari is Muslim, and both of our moms would have a fit if they knew we sometimes indulged in the rare pork product. It's not like either of our families keep strict kosher or halal, but pig is definitely a no-go for them.

"Why Nashville?" I ask.

"Isaac is applying to Vanderbilt, so we figured we'd make a trip of it. I told myself I was actually going to *have fun* this year. Foreign concept, right?" Too right. "Can't believe our parents said yes. I mean, we're staying with Isaac's aunt up there, but still. I guess they're gearing up to take off our training wheels, you know?"

"Yep," I say.

I'm relieved to hear she'll be busy this weekend. Maybe she really is easing back on schoolwork.

The main double doors whoosh open. Dr. Whitmore strides in, and we all straighten in our seats. She looks like a conductor. Black slacks. White blouse. Hair swept up into an orderly bun. She clears her throat and takes the podium. The room drops into taut silence.

I'm pretty sure she hates us, and the feeling is mutual. She doesn't care about anything except making sure we come first in state every year, and she gets away with her harsh methods because the school loves the prestige of those awards.

Last week, a cellist forgot his sheet music. Dr. Whitmore lectured him for five minutes, ironically chiding him for wasting everyone's time. She didn't stop until she brought him to tears. It's why most of us have multiple copies of our sheet music, extras tucked away in our lockers and cars.

But being prepared isn't enough. We have to be perfect.

She doesn't care if our blistered fingers burst and bleed—if she isn't happy with a movement, a meter, or even a note, she'll keep at us, often making us play past the bell, with the one word that terrifies us all: "Again."

A lot of students quit. Tapping out freshman year. Giving in to a concerned parent sophomore year. Saying *screw it, this isn't worth it* junior year. But many others remain. Because the truth is, we also want the prestige. First in state looks damn good on a college application. We're masochists, and Dr. Whitmore knows it.

Pari pulls out the Mozart sheet music. Her nails are coated in chipped orange polish. But then Dr. Whitmore says, "I've prepared something new for us."

She's met with silence. Usually, we get our sheet music over the summer. The runs are so difficult we need plenty of time to practice for fall competition.

"I've decided the Mozart, while darling, isn't difficult enough to truly showcase our talents, so we'll be learning Rimsky-Korsakov's *Scheherazade*. It requires a full orchestra, so some members of the band will be joining our rehearsals later in the semester. Violin section, you're up first. Line up outside my office for the music."

I pinch the bridge of my nose. When the hell am I supposed to make time to learn a new piece? God, I hope there's not a difficult solo.

I stand and follow the section to Dr. Whitmore's office. Masochists.

"Can you believe she's changing the music?" Pari whispers to me. "No one has time for this. Why does every teacher think their class is the most important? I swear I'd drop orchestra if I didn't love playing violin so much. Though, she's doing good work to change that."

Yes, she should drop orchestra. Then I wouldn't have to worry about a better player sitting next to me.

"Yeah, this is rough," I say.

I step up to the desk. Dr. Whitmore focuses in on me. She holds the sheet music just out of my grasp. "Ariel, there is quite a complex solo here." Damn it. "I know you're more than capable of playing up to the challenge. And if you're not, well…"

She lets the sentence hang, then passes the music to me. "Go over the solo now. Third movement," she says. "We'll spend the rest of class doing a run-through."

I walk back to my seat in a daze, staring at the pages. The notes swim before my eyes, but when I get to the solo, they stand in daunting clarity. This is some next-level shit. Doesn't she know we're a high school orchestra and not the Atlanta Symphony?

Pari glances at me as she sits down. "Did you hear she's going to make us run through this today?" I ask.

She sighs. "Yeah, this is going to be hell. I am *not* jealous of that solo. Good luck, buddy."

I give her a forced smile, then turn back to studying the notes. Ten minutes later, everyone settles back into their seats, pencils scratching on the sheet music, fingers running down the necks of instruments. I'm trying to understand the convoluted start of the solo, but even the first few measures refuse to make sense.

Dr. Whitmore takes the stand. "I'm not a monster," she says. Cue a hundred pairs of rolling eyes. "But we are going to run through the piece today. This is a wonderful opportunity for sight-reading practice. We struggled through that portion of the competition last year, and I know we can do better. I don't expect it to be perfect." She gives a sickeningly sweet smile that says otherwise. "And we'll take it at a slow tempo. If we get lost, we'll stop and go again. All right, everyone?"

Like we could say no.

The baton lifts. We set our instruments. The baton drops.

The room bursts with sound. Lyrical yet jagged. Light, high notes. Lilting melodies ending in harsh full stops. The piece is full, beautiful even with our fumbling. My fingers scramble down my violin. At least we're a mess together. Dr. Whitmore jerks the baton up and down roughly, like she can corral us into playing better if she whips it through the air with enough force. I'm counting the time I have left until my solo begins. A few pages. Then lines.

My fingers sweat, almost slipping on the metal strings.

Only measures left. Ten. Five. My bow slips, but my thumb repositions its grip in time to keep it from falling.

Two measures.

My heart pounds.

The room goes quiet and—

My first note is out of tune. My eyes blur as I try to focus on the page. Dr. Whitmore's stare pierces me. I'm supposed to meet her gaze while playing, acknowledge her and her baton, but there's no chance of that with music this new. My fingers fumble like I'm last chair. They squeak out notes one by one, off tempo and out of tune.

It's all I can do to play and breathe.

And then, with a final flat note, it's over, and the entire orchestra raises their instruments to burst back into play. I muster the courage to meet Dr. Whitmore's eyes.

Disdain.

The movement is supposed to continue. But she drops her baton. We put down our instruments.

Silence.

Dr. Whitmore stares right at me. It takes every ounce of nerve not to bolt from the room.

"Well, that won't do," she says, her voice hard. "Ariel, again."

I swallow, throat thick, eyes stinging. She *just* handed out the music. What does she expect?

She lifts the baton. We set our instruments. I play it again.

———————

"Kids, dinner! Wash your hands!" Dad calls from downstairs.

I peel my face off my pillow and blink. I must have crashed when I got home from school. "Ariel? You okay?"

I clear my throat, then sit up, a little light-headed. My sister, Rachel, stands in my doorway. She's in fifth grade, but skipped kindergarten. Her teachers wanted her to skip *three grades*, but my parents said no way. Her hair, dark and curly like the rest of us, is past her shoulders, and she's wearing her favorite tie-dye dress.

"Yeah, I'm good." I rub my face. "Long week. I was resting my eyes."

"Um, yeah, you were definitely snoring. Can we play Scrabble after dinner?"

"Sure." I smile, but there's a knot in my stomach. Dr. Whitmore said I need to perfect the *Scheherazade* solo in two weeks *or else*.

Literally, she said *or else*.

I wash up in my bathroom, then check the notes on my phone, scanning through all the work I need to get done this weekend. The never-ending reading for Spanish lit. My homework for AP Physics. Of course, calculus. I have to get an A on the upcoming test, so I need to dedicate every spare minute to studying for it. The violin solo will have to wait until next week, even with Dr. Whitmore's *or else*.

"Kids!" Dad calls.

"Coming!" I respond.

There's a strict no-phones-at-Shabbat dinner policy, so I drop mine on my bed and follow Rachel downstairs. Mom and Dad are in the kitchen, finishing making dinner. Mom pulls a golden-brown challah from the oven, the delicious smell of fresh baked bread wafting through the kitchen. Dad tosses the salad and adds a flourish of crushed almonds. A roasted chicken sits on the counter.

"Smells amazing, guys," I say. "Need help with anything?"

"Want to grab some dressings?" Dad asks.

"Sure thing." I walk to the fridge and grab everyone's favorites.

"No soup?" Rachel whines.

"Sorry, mamaleh, didn't have time," Mom says. Some Friday nights we have matzo ball soup with dinner because my parents are superhuman, working hard all week and still providing home-cooked meals.

Mom is wearing her pencil skirt from work, but with a worn AC/DC T-shirt. She heads to the table with the Kiddush cup and a bottle of Manischewitz, a sweet kosher wine that basically tastes like grape juice.

Then she grabs two lace kippahs and passes one to Rachel. They walk over to the sink, where we keep the Shabbat candles on the ledge in front of the window so the world can see them from outside. They light the candles and wave their hands in circles in front of their eyes three times before saying the prayer: "Baruch atah adonai eloheinu melech haolam asher kideshanu bemitzvotav vetzivanu lehad-lik ner shel Shabbat."

"Amen," Dad and I say.

We all sit, and Dad blesses the wine. We pass the cup around, all drinking some, even Rachel. A lot of Jewish kids are allowed to have a sip of wine on Shabbat from, like, infancy. And in our family, when we turn fifteen, we're allowed to properly drink for Passover, which means four cups of wine over a four-hour seder. I only got through two and half cups last year before I fell out of my chair laughing and called it quits.

"Ariel, want to do the challah?" Mom asks.

"Sure." I place my hand over the braided bread, then lead our final prayer. It's always comforting saying the familiar Hebrew words together. It lightens me in a way that's hard to explain.

After the prayer, I tear off a giant chunk of bread, then break off bits and throw it around the table so everyone has some.

"So," Mom says, passing the salad bowl my way. "How was everyone's week? Bloopers and highlights."

We're all so busy during the week—Mom chasing a story, Dad researching cases, Rachel with all her extracurricular activities—that Shabbat is usually the first time we can all sit down together. So Mom likes us to catch up by sharing the best parts, and most epic fails, of our weeks.

Rachel tosses a cherry tomato in the air and catches it with her mouth, then grins wide at all of us. "Well!" she says, because she always wants to go first and none of us mind. "I picked my pirate for High Seas week and guess who I get to be? Guess, guess! Okay, I'll tell you. I get to be Ching Shih!"

We all exchange baffled looks. "Who?" I ask.

"*Ching Shih*," Rachel says, exasperated. "The most feared pirate of all time! She was a prostitute in the 1800s, then married a famous pirate, and when he died, she took over and became super-scary and was in charge of, like, everyone."

"Prostitute pirate," Mom says. "That sounds appropriate."

"She's awesome. You'll see. We're doing a whole week of activities. And I'm doing my own two-hour presentation."

"Two hours?" Mom asks.

"With games and stuff! Like a treasure hunt. It's going to be so cool. Our teacher said it's the best part of every year."

"I'm glad you're excited." Dad spears a cucumber. "What about your blooper?"

"Umm…" Rachel bounces her legs and stares at the ceiling like she might find an answer there. "I maybe left the cage door open for the class rabbit, and he maybe ended up in the school-yard trying to burrow under the fence to the road?"

"Rachel, really?" Dad asks.

"Yeah, and you maybe have to sign a note from my teacher saying we talked about personal accountability."

Mom sighs, then smiles and kisses Rachel on the forehead. "Always an adventure with you. Saul, you want to go next?"

Dad tells us about a triumph with an ageism case and then about the coffee he spilled on some important papers, and then Mom tells us about snagging an interview with the new mayor and about getting a ticket for parking on the wrong side of the street. "I swear, they switch it every other week," Mom says. "Who can keep up?"

"Maybe you should have a personal accountability lesson," Rachel says with a smirk.

Mom eyes Rachel, and we all laugh.

"Okay, Ariel," Mom prompts. "Blooper and highlight."

I hesitate. "I almost walked out the door without a shirt on this morning," I say. "Dad saved me."

Rachel laughs, and so does Dad, but Mom looks concerned. "Maybe you need to slow down in the mornings," she says.

"I'm good, Mom. Really."

"You could go to bed earlier. Or go on a shorter run."

I shift in my chair. "I thought it was funny. You were supposed to laugh. It was funny, Dad, right?"

He glances between the two of us. "Yeah, I'm a smart man. I'm not getting in the middle of this."

Mom rolls her eyes. "Honestly, Saul. You're so weak."

"This is true, Miriam," he agrees. "All right, Ariel. Highlight?"

Wow. So many to choose from. I can talk about the calc quiz I failed or the orchestra solo I bombed. I tear my challah into small pieces. The rest of my family doesn't have *real* failures.

They have blunders, gaffes. I'm the only one messing up import-

ant things.

"Ariel?" Mom asks.

I swallow. "Uh, I ran a minute faster than my average this morning."

"Nice." Dad air-high-fives me.

"Proud of you, boychik," Mom says.

"Thanks."

I rip my challah again and again until it crumbles.

THREE

"Barchu et adonai hamvorah," Rabbi Solomon leads.

"Barchu et adonai hamvorah leiolam va-edh," the congregation echoes.

I mumble the response prayer while reading *Crime and Punishment* off my Kindle, which is tucked inside my prayer book and angled away from my parents. I need to devote as much time to calculus as possible without ignoring my other classes, so I'm getting creative.

Mom and Dad are on my left. They're a matched pair, both wearing classic tallit with dark-blue stripes and the identical reading glasses they purchased in a multipack at Costco. Rachel is on my right, paying close attention, reading along with every prayer. She goes to Hebrew School three times a week now and is only a few years away from her bat mitzvah. Before I know it, she'll be in high school, sitting in Ms. Hayes's office.

Mom notices my Kindle. She nudges me and gives *the look*. "Pay attention, Ariel."

We're not the most religious Jews on the kibbutz, but we go to services every Saturday. My parents are machers in the community. Everyone knows and loves them. Sometimes I enjoy services, but when I'm behind on homework, every minute stretches by like an hour.

After reading from the Torah, Rabbi Solomon takes the bema and gives her sermon. There are 613 mitzvot in the Torah, and 74 of those good deeds are in this week's portion. It's a parsha of ethical battlegrounds, about making the right decisions even in the most difficult times.

Rabbi Solomon engages me enough I don't pick up my phone or Kindle for twenty minutes straight. Eventually, though, we switch to Hebrew prayer, and despite the ethical ramifications of reading during services, I dive back into *Crime and Punishment*.

After services, we convene in the social hall for kiddush. Congregants swirl around Mom, noshing on bagels and lox as they schmooze. Mom has this ability to make eye contact with everyone at once. Dad says she's the belle of every ball, even the ones she doesn't attend. It's why she's a great journalist. She's a talented writer, but she also connects with everyone. And if you're friends with someone, they'll come to you with their stories first.

Dad is off in a corner, a raisin bagel in his mouth, not-so-discreetly working on his phone. Rachel is out of sight, probably running around Tinder Hill Park. The wooded trails back up to the synagogue, and after services, kids race around, playing hide-and-seek and tag. Jealousy seethes through me for a second.

"Shabbat Shalom, Ariel."

I turn and find Malka Rothberg wearing her Saturday best. An olive wrap dress hugs her curves, though it goes past her knees and covers her arms. Her dark hair falls in waves against her face, a contrast to her light skin.

We dated for about two seconds when I was a rising sophomore and she was a rising junior, but it was one of those relationships people have just so they can say they were in a relationship. We're much better off as friends. She goes to college in Atlanta now.

"Good Shabbos," I say. "What's up? How's school?"

"School is good…" She trails off. "Commuting back and forth for the band can be a pain, but it's okay." Malka plays guitar in Sook's band, Dizzy Daisies, and drives back to our suburb all the time for practice.

I nod. "Cool, cool." I glance at the door. I need to leave soon. I have a volunteer shift at the animal shelter. Hopefully I'll be able to get some studying done there.

Malka narrows her eyes. "You okay?"

"Yep." I scratch the back of my head. My fingers meet the bobby pin holding my kippah in place. I slide both off and shove them in my pocket. "So are Sook and I going to lose you to the cool, glamorous life of college?"

She laughs, awkwardly, and tucks a lock of hair behind her ear. "Yup. I'm too cool for you seventeen-year-olds."

"Dude, you turned eighteen a month ago."

"Dude, whatever." She grins. "Hey! You should join us for practice sometime. Sook wrote a new song that would sound great with violin."

"I'll think about it. No promises."

It would be nice to play violin for fun again, but I don't have the time for that. My alarm goes off, phone buzzing in my pocket. "I've gotta go. Animal shelter. I'll see you soon. Tell me some cool-kid college stories next time, okay?"

She laughs awkwardly again. I give her a quick hug and head out.

"Ezekiel, come back!" I shout, chasing after the loose terrier. I didn't knot his leash properly before bathing him, and now he's running around the back of the shelter, a tiny ball of suds and fury. "Get him, Rachel!"

"On it!" She scampers after him. She forgot a change of

clothes, so she's wearing one of my T-shirts over her Shabbos dress. It hangs down to her knees. Ezekiel stops at the window to bark at a squirrel. Rachel sneaks up behind him and pulls him to her chest with a gentle hug. He scrambles for a second, but then gives in and kisses her face. "Good boy." She giggles.

"Thank you, hero sister." I help her settle Ezekiel back into the giant sink, then scrub him while he licks my hand.

"Any time!"

I've been volunteering at this animal shelter for two years. Volunteer work is a must for a good college application, and this place is an easy shtick. The manager, Marnie, has an overflowing roster of volunteers: animal rights activists, college students, and retirees. She doesn't actually need me, so I keep spare clothes in the car and only come once a week after synagogue.

It's hard to watch the animals stuck in these cages, but at least when I'm here, I can let them out and run around with them. And they especially love it when I bring Rachel. "Watch this!" she shouts.

She's trained a mutt that's definitely part standard poodle to jump up on its hind legs and beg for a treat. The dog is almost taller than her when it does so. "Badass," I say.

She bows. "Thank you. Now we can tell her future parents she's well trained."

I grin. "Yeah, but is she housebroken?"

Rachel shrugs and gives a mischievous smile before turning

her attention back to the dog. An hour later, we're done with the washing and the walks, and I tell Rachel, "I've got to study. You gonna play in the yard?"

Rachel sighs. "I've got to study, too, big brother."

I raise my eyebrow. "Study for what?"

"Geography," she says. "We have a test on the capitals."

"Oh, that won't be bad," I say.

"Capitals of all the countries."

"What?" We didn't do that until ninth grade. Though I'd be no help to her now. It's the kind of information you forget a week after you learn it.

"It's multiple choice," Rachel says, which is better, I guess. "Can Ezekiel study with me?"

"Sure."

Rachel grabs Ezekiel from his kennel, and we head to the front of the shelter. I sit at the desk, and Rachel sits on the entryway couch, dwarfed by the backpack next to her. It's a slow Saturday, so we're the only ones here at the moment. Ezekiel curls up on the floor near Rachel's feet. She's bent over an open folder, studying while munching on a bag of Cheetos.

I take out my notebook, my calc textbook, and a bag of Sour Patch Kids. I chew on the sour candy while copying down the first problem. My pencil carves deep grooves in the paper, like if I write the numbers hard enough, the formulas will stick in my brain. Then I flip to the front of the chapter to study the steps. My shoulders hunch over the page. A stress headache blooms in my forehead. It takes far too long to do one problem, but finally I have it. A wave of relief sweeps over me. I flip to the back of the book to confirm my answer is right.

It's not.

Crap.

It's too warm for soccer season. The bright sun beats down on me as I climb out of my car. The Grateful Dead plays through my phone speakers. A light breeze ruffles the air but doesn't offset the humid heat.

My family is already at the field. They came early to set up the tent and food because the parents in this area like to tailgate elementary school soccer games like it's college football. I peer down on the scene from the top of the hill.

The fields back up to the same trails as my synagogue, all of Tinder Hill Park. I'd love to spend the day watching Rachel's game, then walking the trails with Sook, but I brought my own car so I could come late and peace out early to study. The final hours of the weekend are ticking down, and I'm nowhere near ready for this test next Friday.

I glance at my phone. 11:27. Only twelve hours left in the day, fifteen if I make it a late night.

I head down the hill toward my parents, who are congregated

with Amir's family. We sit together every game. Rasha, Amir's older sister, laughs loudly at some joke my dad must have cracked. She's wearing a black blouse and a lavender hijab. Her parents are next to her, digging into the food with my mom, piling plates high with pasta salad, cold chicken tikka, and cut-up fruit.

Amir is off on his own, down the sideline, taking pictures as everyone warms up for the game. He's on one knee, back bent at an odd angle, neck craned. I wonder if the exaggerated pose is contrived, like he's paying more attention to what he looks like than what the photo looks like.

Mrs. Naeem calls my name and waves me over. She doesn't look a day over thirty, even though she has a twenty-year-old daughter. Unlike Rasha, she doesn't wear a hijab, so her dark hair is loose around her shoulders.

"Hi, Mrs. Naeem." I say.

"Beta, come here!" She gives me a hug. Then I shake Mr. Naeem's hand and wave at Rasha, who cuts off conversation with my dad to come over and say hi.

"How's college going?" I ask her.

"Slow. The start of the semester is boring. Too many people dropping and adding classes to get anything done. Total waste of time." Rasha yawns. "God, it's early."

"It's eleven thirty," Mrs. Naeem says. "You're not a teenager anymore—no more sleeping until two in the afternoon."

"I take late classes," Rasha says.

Mrs. Naeem tsks, and Rasha rolls her eyes.

Even though she's in college, she still lives at home. She lived on campus in the dorms freshman year, but said she missed being around her family. Especially Sara. She wants to be there while her little sister grows up.

"Ariel's always been a morning person," Mom says. Actually, this is not true. I force myself to be a morning person. I can't remember the last time I woke up without an alarm. Even this summer, I woke up early to study for the SATs. I'd already scored a 1560, but I wanted that perfect 1600.

And I got it.

"I'm jealous," Mrs. Naeem responds.

"Don't be. If they're asleep, they can't beg you to make them breakfast on the weekends."

I nudge Mom's shoulder and grin. "I'm very sorry you have to feed your child."

She nudges back. "You're seventeen. You can make your own breakfast when I want to sleep in on a Saturday."

"But you do it so well," I respond. Still, I feel a twinge of guilt. Mom works hard all week. I don't like bothering her with homework woes, and I shouldn't bother her to make me scrambled eggs, either.

"Come here," she says. "You have some schmutz."

Before I have a chance to get away, she licks her finger and rubs my cheek. "*Mom*."

"Oh, hush, tatala."

The ref blows his whistle, and we all turn toward the field. Rachel and Sara both play forward, center and right. The wind picks up, whistling through the trees, and clouds move in and dampen the sun.

My phone buzzes. Sook: *Want to hang after Rachel's game?*

Maybe I could walk around Tinder Hill for an hour. I'm about to text back when my parents yell, "Go, go, go!"

My gaze snaps to the field. Rachel passes the ball to Sara, and they both sprint forward, eluding the other team's defense. Adrenaline rushes through me. I feel transported onto the field, like I'm the one dribbling the ball and tearing past the players. I clench my fist and lean forward. "C'mon," I murmur. "C'mon."

Sara rushes the goal, strikes the ball, and—

"GOAL!" I shout as the ball sails cleanly into the net. Everyone erupts in cheers, and I pump my fist into the air.

But the adrenaline drains fast, as I remember my own days of playing are over. My place is on the sidelines now.

The remainder of the first half goes by in a blur. The other team is one of the best in the area, so they actually give our girls a challenge, keeping the game interesting. At halftime, we all turn to the food. I'm piling my plate high with chicken and fruit when Mrs. Naeem asks, "So, Ariel, how are college applications going? Where are you applying again?"

I scratch the back of my neck, my shoulders tense.

"Harvard," Dad says, patting me on the back. "Smart kid. I'm sure he'll get in."

"I don't know, Dad," I say.

"That's wonderful, Ariel!"

I force a smile and say thanks, but then quickly bow out of the conversation. I used to talk about applying to Harvard as if it were inevitable, the next logical step in my education. But classes have gotten more difficult. I'm barely scraping As, and now with that failed quiz…

Am I Harvard material? Or am I only good at signing up for the right classes? Pari is smarter. I'm just better at working the system. Soon that might not be enough. And the more people my parents tell about Harvard, the more people will know I'm a fraud when I don't get in.

I stroll down the sideline until I'm a few dozen feet past the field and alone. I click open my phone and pull up the CalcU app, looking at practice problems I've already gone through multiple times. Last night, I was three pages deep into Google results searching for extra problems.

I pinch the bridge of my nose. Damn it.

I used to *like* school. That burst of satisfaction when new material clicks. The competitive gratification of finishing a test first, knowing you got everything right. But there's nothing to enjoy when a failing grade is staring you in the face. Maybe Ms. Hayes is right. Maybe I should get a tutor.

I'm about to turn on my *Crime and Punishment* audiobook when I hear someone walk up behind me. Spearmint and basil. Instinctively, I inhale.

I turn to find Amir. He's wearing a T-shirt with the Ravenclaw house sigil on it. He *would* identify as Ravenclaw, the most pretentious of the Hogwarts houses.

"Hey," I say. "Do my parents need something?"

"Uh, no." He looks awkward. Amir Naeem actually looks awkward. "Sorry, I was coming to...hang out."

Hang out? We don't hang out.

"Never mind." He shakes his head. "I'll go over there."

"It's okay," I say, surprising myself. "We can hang."

"All right." He rocks on his heels. "I hate the college talk."

"Yeah, same. That's why I left."

Amir smiles. "Great minds think alike and all that. It's incessant. If I have to hear one more overt hint that I should go to some liberal arts school—"

"Don't you want to? Or wait, do you want to skip college and, like, move to Brooklyn and live in a loft?"

Amir raises his eyebrow. "Hmm."

"Erm, sorry," I say. "That sounded judgy, didn't it?"

Amir laughs. "Little bit. But it's okay." He shrugs. "College isn't for everyone, but I'm definitely going. I want to be a doctor, and I'm almost positive doctors have to go to medical school."

"A doctor? Not a photographer?"

"Ariel, you sound like my parents." My stomach flips when he says my name. A slight smile plays on his lips. "Photography is a hobby. I'm also passionate about medicine, but it's not like I can carry around a scalpel and fix aortic dissections on frogs."

"Well, I guess you *could*," I say. "But it probably wouldn't end well."

I laugh, and so does Amir. His brown eyes are warm, and when they meet with mine, my stomach doesn't just flip again, it does full-fledged Olympic-level gymnastics.

I look down for a moment, my skin hot. "So why a doctor?"

Amir hesitates. "I don't want to say."

"C'mon. What?"

"It's going to sound silly. Cheesy." He runs a hand through his dark hair. The silk strands glint in the sun.

"Try me."

"Fine, okay." He takes a breath. "I can go to school and learn how to save lives. I can get a *degree* in saving lives. How wild is that? Medicine is a miracle, and I want to be a part of it."

I can feel it, the passion he has, the optimism. It radiates from him. For years, I've had one goal in mind. Get into Harvard. I've been focused on acceptance, not what I'll actually study there. But for Amir, acceptance isn't the end goal—it's just a step toward something greater.

"I think it's amazing," I say. "Of course, it's amazing."

"Thanks," Amir responds. He scratches his stubble. "Hey, can I show you a picture?"

"Uh, sure."

He steps forward and turns so we're standing side by side. We're about the same height. He maybe has an inch on me. His broad shoulders brush against mine, and my cheeks heat as I wonder what he'd look like without his Ravenclaw shirt on.

I clear my throat and concentrate on his Nikon camera. "I think this is a nice shot of the girls," Amir says, voice calm, unaffected by our closeness.

Sara is kicking the ball into the goal, and Rachel is rushing forward, screaming something, probably "applesauce," which she thinks is hilarious because it always confuses the defense.

"Awesome photo," I say. "You're pretty good at this."

"I know," Amir says with a small smile. It's not a brag, simply confidence. He's sure of his talent. I know that feeling, like when I'm on a roll with classes, and all the assignments churn out one after another, and I know I'm earning As. It's an assuredness, a certainty, I miss. "I can print a copy for your family if you want."

"I'm sure Rachel would love that. A small one, though—her ego is big enough."

Amir grins. "Noted."

"It's nice of you," I say, "photographing all the games."

"Happy to do it. They're good memories to have. Our sisters are pretty awesome."

A lot of my friends think it's weird to be close to their siblings. They see them as annoying people ·who share their houses and nothing more. But I love Rachel, and it's cool Amir gets that.

He glances past me, at the field. "The second half will start soon. Should we head back?"

I hadn't realized that much time had passed. I'm pretty sure this is the longest conversation I've ever had with Amir. I always thought he had no interest in speaking to me, but maybe he thought I had no interest in speaking to him. He's kind of nice to be around. I guess it's not so bad he's the one who graded my quiz.

The quiz he passed with flying colors.

Wait…

Amir is walking back when I call out, "Hey, could you, um, do me a favor?"

"Graduation photos?"

"Uh, no, not that." I take a short breath. "You did really well on that math quiz." He seems to be waiting for an actual question, so I blurt out, "Do you think you could tutor me in calc? I can pay you. Well, I can pay you when Hanukkah rolls around."

"I don't want your money."

Oh. Good. I've embarrassed myself and still don't have a tutor.

"Come over tomorrow night and we'll study together."

Oh. *Oh.* "Really?"

He nods. "It's not a problem. C'mon, let's go watch our kick-ass sisters."

As we head back toward our families, relief floods through me. Maybe this will turn out okay. I glance at Amir, and he smiles at me, eyes shining in the light.

Maybe this will turn out more than okay.

FOUR

"Problems twenty-seven to forty-eight for homework," Mr. Eller says as the bell rings. Everyone stands and gathers their books. Amir swings his backpack over his shoulder and nods at me. I give a half smile back. I'm not sure why he agreed to help me, but we're studying together at his place tonight, and hopefully it'll go well.

It has to go well.

Pari turns to me. "Coming?" she asks.

Isaac stands next to her, his arm draped around her shoulder. Their relationship has always been chaotic, more breakups and reunions than I can count, but they seem solid this year. All my "relationships" have started and ended during summer, quick flirtations before classes gear back up. I've never quite had the time to get comfortable with someone.

"Um, y'all go ahead." I twist my pencil in my hands. "I have to send an email."

"Okay!" Pari smiles. She leans into Isaac, and he pulls her closer. My heart lurches a bit. I could have that with someone, if I wanted it, if I prioritized it over my grades. But good grades will get me into a good school. And a good school will get me a good job. And a good job will get me a good life.

It *does* matter. It's ridiculous to think otherwise.

I pull out my phone while the classroom clears, my leg shaking up and down. I click to the Harvard Admissions page, scrolling through staged photos of happy students and application requirements. I should prepare more for my interview. It's not the most important part of the application, but still, I need to convince Hannah that Harvard and I are the perfect fit.

When the classroom is empty, I grab my backpack and walk to Mr. Eller's desk, my pulse racing. He's flipping through a folder of papers. "Where on earth did I put that…" he mumbles.

Seems like his life is as haphazard as his teaching. Mr. Eller always jumps from one point to another, never going straight through a problem. I wish my teacher from last year taught BC also. I wouldn't call AB easy, but it was manageable with her as a teacher.

It's amazing so many kids are doing well in this class. Though, maybe it's only Amir, and everyone else is faking it along with me. Maybe Pari is bright and cheery because she's playing my same game.

"Mr. Eller," I say. "Do you have a moment?"

His eyes are unfocused when he glances up at me. "Mm-hmm, yes, what is it, Ariel?"

"AR-riel," I correct, with the hard pirate *arrr*.

He lifts his hand. "All right."

I grab a strap of my backpack and loop it around my hand again and again until the constriction turns the skin white. "I was wondering," I say, releasing the strap, "if you would give me partial credit for correcting my quiz answers."

He doesn't hesitate. "No." He leans forward. "If you get the problem wrong, you get it wrong and study harder next time."

My throat tightens, as pressure builds behind my eyes. I take a breath, but it's too shallow. He couldn't care less about my grade, about me. I've spent more than three years asking teachers about extra credit and corrections. Sometimes they say yes, and sometimes they say no, but none have felt quite as dismissive as Mr. Eller.

If only he knew how much I need this.

If only he knew that one quiz threatens more than three years of relentless work.

I swallow hard and muster on. "What about extra credit? I could complete some extra practice problems or—"

"Ariel, no." He says my name wrong again. The pressure

keeps building behind my eyes. *Don't cry. It's only a grade.* But the thought just makes it worse.

"The grades you get are the grades you get. I'm simply trying to prepare you kids for the real world. There aren't do-overs in life. You still have plenty of time to pull up your grade. If you need a tutor, I encourage you to check out the sign-up sheets in the guidance office."

"Right, okay," I manage to say. "Thanks."

"Glad to help."

He's already bent back over his papers. I escape the classroom, rubbing my eyes before any tears can escape.

"Want some?" Sook asks.

She pulls lotion out of her purse. It's one of those expensive kinds in an aluminum tube. We're sitting on top of our desks in AP Lit, waiting for the bell to ring. *Crime and Punishment* is open in front of me, but I'm not actually reading it. I no longer feel tense. Instead, I'm drained, exhausted.

There's no extra credit. Studying on my own didn't work. If tutoring with Amir doesn't help, I don't know what I'll do.

"Ariel?"

"Yeah, thanks," I say. She squeezes a drop onto my hands. I rub them together and inhale. Lavender and the slightest scent of basil. My cheeks warm.

"You didn't text me back yesterday," she says, crossing her legs. She's wearing a long off-white blouse and expensive tan leggings that look more suitable for dressage than school.

"I didn't? Crap, sorry. What was it again?"

"I wanted to hang out with my best friend. I'm starting to forget what his face looks like."

"Sook, we drive to school together every morning and have two classes together."

"Yeah, but that doesn't count. And you're on your phone like ninety-five percent of the drive. Come over tonight. I have something exciting to tell you!"

"You could tell me now."

"Boo, no. The fluorescent lights will kill the joy of it. C'mon. We can watch the new Marvel movie and eat peanut butter fudge cupcakes."

"Damn, that sounds nice."

This past summer I upped my hours at the animal shelter and also helped out at the Jewish Community Center day camp, but all my free time was spent with Sook. We walked the trails in Tinder Hill Park, listening to music and smoking the occasional joint. We had a *Great British Bake Off* bake-a-thon, where for two weeks straight we binged the show and tried to copy their recipes. And we went to concerts all over Atlanta: a cover band of the Beatles at a tiny venue, an orchestra concert at the Atlanta Symphony, and a punk show at some dark, dingy basement that made me want a tetanus shot. But since school started, I've barely seen her outside of it.

"C'mon," Sook says. "I have shrimp snacks."

I inhale. "Really?"

She nods. "Really."

Shrimp snacks are crunchy chips with delicious seasoning that taste like getting into Heaven. Sook gets them and more of her favorite Korean snacks whenever her parents drive to Buford Highway.

"I'm sorry. I can't. I have plans already."

Her eyes narrow. "Plans with who?"

"Uh, nothing. No one. An extra shift at the animal shelter."

The lie slides out with ease, then a twinge of guilt. I don't lie to Sook. I don't lie much in general. But if I tell my best friend I'm failing, she'll be concerned and ask questions and try to help, and this façade of having my shit together will collapse.

I'll study with Amir, bring up my grade, and no one has to know I slipped.

The bell rings.

We both take our seats. I pull out my Ticonderoga #2 pencil from behind my ear and flip to a fresh page of my spiral notebook.

I'm probably the least-organized valedictorian in history, using the same jumbo notebook for all my classes until it runs out of space and I have to start a new one. It's easier that way, less stuff to bring home. All my notes from the week are in one place, and when finals come around, I shrug sheepishly and ask Sook if I can photocopy her notes because mine are a hot mess. It's best friend symbiosis because she always copies forgotten homework assignments from me.

Mrs. Rainer strides into the room. She's awesome, and Sharon Mo, last year's valedictorian, swore her class was an easy A. Mrs. Rainer's white hair is streaked with pink, and glasses dangle from a chain around her neck.

"Morning, class." She unzips her black fanny pack, which is covered in glitter and gemstones, and takes out a dry-erase marker. *Got to keep them close*, she said on the first day of class, *these things always seem to disappear to other classrooms.*

The top left of the board reads *Daily Writing Prompt* in permanent marker. We do a quick-write for five minutes every morning. Mrs. Rainer says creativity needs a warm-up like our muscles.

"Hmm," she says, then writes: *Apple pie with vanilla ice cream.*

A couple kids laugh, and Mrs. Rainer gives us a look. "What? I'm hungry, okay? All right, all right. Simmer down. Five minutes. Let's go."

I crack my neck, titling my head to the left then right. The classroom is silent, save the light scratching of pens and pencils. With no grade attached, the words flow out easily.

Rebecca kneaded the piecrust dough while her mom peeled apples. "We should put chili powder in!" Rebecca said.

"Ew, Rebecca no!"

"What about oregano?"

"Definitely not."

"Pepper?"

"Honestly, who taught you how to bake?"

"You did!"

"Please don't tell people that."

Before I know it, Mrs. Rainer calls, "Time! Pencils down! Okay, who wants to read their story out loud?"

I close my notebook. Definitely not. My unpolished writing is embarrassing, especially because half the people in this class can basically craft the opening of a novel in, like, five minutes. Ellen Cho raises her hand and reads off her story about an apple pie baking contest. After compliment and critique, Mrs. Rainer turns on the smart board and clicks away at her computer.

"All right, class," she says. "Today, I thought we'd go over a college essay. Keep in mind, our *Crime and Punishment* essay test is coming up at the end of next week. We'll begin to go over the text tomorrow, all right? Now! This is from a student of mine a couple of years ago. He got into Princeton."

I slump down into my seat, stomach twisting. I still haven't started my college essay. More likely than not, I'll write about playing violin, but thousands and thousands of applicants are in orchestra. There's nothing special about it. It's not a true *passion*. Maybe I could lie and say I compose my own music, but an admissions counselor could probably fact-check that.

I wish I had a real passion like everyone else. Sook has her band. Amir has his camera. Everyone has something that makes them stand out. Everyone except me.

When I signed up for classes freshman year, no one told me that straight As, volunteer hours, and time in the arts aren't enough. No one told me I'd have to know every answer to every test and also be a "unique individual" following my life's calling at seventeen.

"Want to come over after the animal shelter?" Sook whispers as Mrs. Rainer searches her computer. "We can eat shrimp snacks and work on our essays."

I stare down at my blank page.

"Yeah," I say. "That would be good."

I text Amir: *I'm here*

A minute later, I'm walking up to the door as it opens. Amir stands in front of me, wearing gray sweatpants and a plain white V-neck. His stubble is dark and runs over his cheeks and along the curve of his sharp jaw. My eyes scan him a moment too long, and the word *want* surfaces in my thoughts.

He cracks a crooked smile. "Hey."

"Hey. So—"

"So—"

We both laugh. Amir scratches the back of his neck, still grinning. "So, okay. Come on in. I'm set up in the kitchen."

"Yeah, sounds good."

His house is familiar. Art hangs on the walls, from prints of famous artists to Amir's photography to Rasha's watercolors. Sara has her own nook, shelves full of pottery and photos from ballet and soccer. We head down the hall to the kitchen. The table sits by a giant bay window overlooking the backyard.

Amir mentioned his family is out watching Sara's play. He already went to opening night. "Would you like a drink?" he asks. He opens the fridge and leans over it, one arm pressed against the frame. I try and fail not to stare at his bicep. "We have Coke, iced tea, water…"

"Tea works," I say.

Amir pours us both a cup, then grabs a bag of chips and some grapes. I pull out sour gummy worms and Haribo Fizzy Cola bottles from my backpack. He laughs when he sees them and asks, "Sour candy fan?"

"Understatement of the year," I respond. Honestly, I don't know how I'd get anything done without sour candy.

We go to settle at the table, but there are a bunch of photos spread out over it. "Sorry," Amir says, sliding them into a pile. I catch a glimpse of Rasha in a library and a photo of their parents laughing in the kitchen.

"Can I see that one?" I ask, reaching for it.

"Sure."

Amir hands it to me. It's an evocative shot, within a private moment. It feels as if they're alone in the room. Intimacy caught on film.

Something stirs in me. "It's really good."

"Do you think so? I can't figure out which ones to use."

"Use for what?"

"A competition for high school photographers. If you win, your work gets shown in this new art gallery. It's not the best space, but still, I'd have my photographs on an actual gallery wall." His eyes light up. "And they're giving scholarship money. I can only pick five pieces for my application, so I've narrowed it down to shots of the family, but..." He stacks the photos. There must be at least two hundred of them. "I have a few of those." He raises his eyebrows, looking a little overwhelmed.

I nod. "Quite a few."

"They're good subjects. There's something familiar and unfamiliar about looking at your family through a lens, seeing your parents as actual people." His fingers trace the photo of them. "Capturing a moment I wouldn't linger on otherwise."

"Like Sunday mornings," I say, half to myself.

"Hmm?" Amir glances at me.

I clear my throat, a bit embarrassed. "Sunday mornings at my house. My parents run around nonstop all week, but they have a date at home every Sunday morning. They stay in their pajamas and read the newspaper and sip coffee for hours. And they talk about politics and movies and their friends. It's always weird seeing them like that, like an out-of-body experience, because suddenly they're not Mom and Dad—they're real people."

"I know exactly what you mean," Amir says. "I remember the first time I really *saw* my dad." He leans forward some, and I do, too. My skin tingles. "I was fourteen. He was running late, and his car wouldn't start, so he got out to check on the engine and spilled coffee on his shirt. And then his boss was calling on the phone, and Sara was cranky and crying, and I thought, *He's really stressed out. It must be tough.* Before that, he was Dad. Invincible. After, he was just a guy."

"It's life-altering when you realize your parents are human."

Amir's gaze connects with mine, and I'm startled by its intensity. But eventually, he looks away, straightening the stack of photos. "So—"

"So—"

We both smile. Amir continues, "We should study. My family will be back in a couple of hours."

"Oh, right." I pause. "Could you not tell them? About the tutoring?" He almost looks hurt, so I quickly continue. "Sorry, it's those human parents of mine. I don't want them finding out I failed a quiz and getting all parent-y." I pick at my nail. "Do you mind? I mean, it's not really lying, more like omitting, but I don't want to get you in trouble."

He's silent for a moment, then says, "Sure. No problem."

Tension eases from my muscles. "It's not like we're sneaking around doing drugs or having sex."

My cheeks burn. Amir said "sex" so casually. I mean, I guess there's a good chance he's had sex. He dates older guys, which means college guys now. And plenty of people have sex in high school, too.

Even though I want to have sex in the abstract, every time I think about *actually* having it, I go into a panic spiral, which tells me I'm not ready. I mean, I know *how* to put on a condom, but what if it's more difficult than it looks? What size do I buy? And do I buy them, or would Amir? I mean, not Amir. I mean—who would buy them? And how do you know your parents aren't going to show up while you're doing it? And—

Yeah, way too stressful. I'll figure it out in college.

I open my textbook and stare at the page. "Where should we start?"

"Math builds on itself, so we need a solid foundation. Let's start at the beginning."

Amir's *we* is generous since *he* obviously has the foundation down.

"Okay, from the beginning then."

I slip my phone out of my pocket and turn off the buzzer so we aren't disturbed. I have three email notifications. What if they're from colleges? No, I need to study. I resist the urge to touch the icon. I'll check when I use the bathroom or something.

We flip to page one. "A heads-up, I've never done this before." Amir sounds confident. It's more a perfunctory notice. "I looked up some how-to guides and—"

I bite back a smile. "You did?"

He shrugs. "Sure."

"That was nice."

"It's no problem. Anyways, tutors make good money. If I take to it, I can charge other people, maybe save some for college."

Oh. Right. "That's good," I say. "Smart."

"I'm going to teach through doing. I'll talk through my work as I complete the problem. Stop me if you have any questions. We'll do a few problems like that and then work on one together. Then you'll take over. That work?"

My pulse races, and my hands grow damp. This is happening. A minute ago it was iced tea and conversation, but now it's on. There's a test in three days. If this study session doesn't work out…

It has to work out.

I grip the edge of my chair and nod, trying to keep my voice level. "Yeah, cool."

Amir angles his notebook toward me and brings his pencil to the page. I don't recognize the brand. It's nice. Like it's from an art supply store, not Office Depot. The graphite slides across the paper. His flicks numbers on the page with ease, his voice soft and steady, explaining each step as promised. I'm so entranced, it takes me a few seconds to realize I'm paying attention to the cadence of his voice not the actual lesson.

"Wait, can you go back?" I ask.

He glances at me. "Sure, to which part?"

I'm too embarrassed to say, "To the beginning," so instead I say, "That last part, the uh—"

"Reversing the inequality?"

"Yeah, that."

He goes back and scrawls the numbers again. "Got it?"

I grip my pencil. "Yep. Thanks."

"I'm glad this is working out."

My grip tightens. "Yeah, me too."

Twenty minutes later, I'm completely lost, but Amir thinks all is well. He flips the page and says, "Okay, so why don't you work through this one, and if you get stuck, I'll help."

I nod. "Sure."

Yeah. Sure.

I take my time copying the problem, checking each and every number before writing it down in my notebook. Then I nibble the end of my eraser, looking it over. My foot shakes up and down.

"Okay," I say. "So apply the quotient rule."

"Right."

Right…

Wait, what's the quotient rule?

Amir just did this. Like, five times in a row. So I can, too. It's only math. I've been doing it forever. One step at a time.

First step, first step…

Oh, right. I deconstruct the first bit of the problem. "Good, right," Amir says.

I pick at my nail. Then bite at my nail.

"Next you'll want to take out the constant," Amir says.

My brain hurts. It actually pulsates.

I take another sip of my tea, but the cup is empty. "Want a refill?" I ask Amir. "I'm kind of thirsty."

"Don't you want to finish the problem?"

"In a second." I stand and grab both of our cups. My pulse skips, staccato. Calm down, Ariel. Focus on something else. His cup has the Deathly Hallows symbol on it. "So you're a big Harry Potter fan, yeah?" I ask him.

"I am," Amir says. "Still waiting on my Hogwarts letter."

"I bet they don't have calculus at Hogwarts."

"They don't, but I've heard Arithmancy is difficult."

My laugh disorients me. It's as if my mind is functioning in two separate spaces. I push toward the good space. "You're a bit of a nerd, aren't you?"

Amir grins. "Little bit."

I turn back, then open the fridge and inhale the cold air. I can do this.

What if I can't do this?

I blink, eyes blurring. I have the distinct urge to break into tears. Stop it. Refocus. I slip out my phone and scan my messages. There's one from Sook: *What time are you coming over?*

I don't respond yet because I have no clue when we'll be done.

"You see it?" Amir asks. "It's on the top shelf."

I shove my phone back into my pocket. "Yeah, thanks." I pour our teas and head back to the table. "What time are your parents coming home again?"

"We have plenty of time. I don't think the first act is even over."

I nod, twisting my fingers together. "What's the play about?"

"A children's adaptation of *Cyrano de Bergerac*. It was pretty funny."

"Oh, I liked that play." My fingers lock together, squeeze. "I'm not loving *Crime and Punishment*. Are you in Mrs. Rainer's class?"

"I am," Amir says, but he doesn't seem interested in more conversation. "C'mon, let's get back to work. We were doing well."

Hah. We really weren't.

I pick up my pencil. The eraser is half-gnawed off.

"Okay," Amir says, "So you were about to take the constant out and—"

"Isn't Mr. Eller the worst teacher?" I ask.

"He's all right. Scattered. So we take out the constant and—"

"I had no problem with calculus last year, but this guy can't teach to save his pension. Good thing he doesn't have to. It's ridiculous. I wish they could get rid of him. Sticking us with this guy at the end of school is such bullshit."

"I guess so. Okay—"

"And he doesn't even—"

"Ariel, stop procrastinating."

His tone is relaxed, but my whole body tenses. He can't see me falter. No one can. I swallow hard, then say, "I'm not procrastinating. I wanted to talk. Sorry. Didn't mean to bother you."

"You aren't bothering me. I *like* talking with you." He pauses. "But you came to me for help, and I want to make sure you get it. If you're still having trouble with the material, we can go back to the beginning." His tone is warm, but I don't feel comforted.

"I don't think this is working out." I close my notebook.

"Wait, what?"

"I don't need this."

My heart pounds fast as I stuff my things into my bag.

"You don't need what?" Amir asks. I stand, and so does he. "You're leaving? Ariel, why?"

"This isn't working for me. I'll be better off studying on my own. Thanks for trying."

"I don't understand what just happened. Sit down. We'll try again."

"No thanks. This was a mistake."

I slip my bag over my shoulder and walk toward the door. If I stay any longer, he'll see what's happening. He'll see I don't understand. I'm not smart enough. I'm an imposter. If I'm going to lose everything I've worked for, at least I don't have to do it in front of an audience.

"Ariel—" he says again.

But the slamming door cuts off his voice.

FIVE

The neighborhood rushes by as my feet smack the pavement. Sweat pours down the back of my neck. My breath comes sharp and fast, while Keith Moon pummels drums for "Who Are You."

My legs ache. My lungs constrict.

I push harder, bearing down, increasing my run to almost a sprint. Wind rushes through my hair. My body floods with endorphins.

Then revolts.

My stomach lurches as I round the corner to my street. I stop short and fling out an arm to brace myself against a tree. I tense, then bend over and dry-heave. But I must have stopped in time because nothing comes up.

I lean against the tree, breathing hard. The song switches to "Happy Jack," and I click down the volume. School starts in less than an hour. I need to get back home, eat breakfast, and try to cram in a bit of extra studying before Sook picks me up. It's like I lost a day trying to study with Amir. I shouldn't have snapped like that. The pressure built too fast, and I turned on the one person who could help me out of this situation.

My stomach lurches for a different reason.

I take a deep breath, then turn the music back up and keep running.

"Are you going to apologize?" Sook asks.

We've been in the car for five minutes, but I've been immersed in the CalcU app. "Huh?" I look up. Sook's hair is swept up into a bun, and she's wearing clear-framed glasses. Her nails tap the steering wheel. "Apologize to who?"

"Um, to your best friend, for ditching our plans yesterday and not even texting me back. I was worried, you know. I almost texted Rachel."

"Oh, crap." I run a hand through my hair. "I spaced out. I'm sorry. I've been busy with…" I trail off. "I forgot. I'm a jerk, and I'm sorry."

"Didn't you get my texts?"

"I saw one…" I have this bad habit of ignoring messages when I'm stressed. They just sit there, stacking up on my phone. "I didn't read them. I'm the worst."

"Yeah, well, you are." She sighs and runs a finger over her eyebrow, smoothing it down.

"I'm sorry, really," I repeat. "How can I make it up to you?"

Sook twists her mouth. "Tinder Hill date this afternoon? I can tell you my news, finally! And I'm working on a new song that could use special *inspiration*." There's a devious glint in her eye. Inspiration means pot. It *can* make music pretty freaking magical.

With this upcoming test, I don't have free time, but this is my best friend, and I did ditch her. "Sure, yeah. Right after school, though, okay? And what is this news of yours?"

"You'll have to wait until this afternoon." Sook nods. "We'll pick up some inspiration from my dealer on the way."

Sook's dealer is the least sketchy person to ever sell drugs. A hippie in her midthirties, Beatrice grows a small crop of marijuana alongside her favorite wildflowers and legal herbs. This past summer, she gifted lavender berry teabags with every purchase.

Sook turns on to the main road.

"Is everything okay with you?" she asks.

The calculus test is Friday. If I fail, it will literally be impossible to get an A in the class. If I don't get an A in the class, I won't have a perfect record. If I don't have a perfect record, I'll be a less appealing applicant for Harvard. If I'm a less appealing applicant for Harvard, I won't get in. If I don't get in—

"Ariel?"

I clear my throat and muster a small smile. "I'm great. Totally great."

I spend math class biting a hangnail and using the sum total of my concentration to avoid eye contact with Amir. I want to apologize, but if I apologize, I'll have to explain, at least partially, what's going on with me. And if I tell someone that this failed quiz could rewrite my entire future, the situation will become more real than I can handle.

When the bell rings, Amir stands and slips out of the classroom before I can close my notebook. Perhaps he's also on Mission Avoid Eye Contact. As I gather my things, Mr. Eller calls me forward, beckoning with a single finger.

Dread curls in my gut. Most of my classmates are still in the room. I feel their eyes on me, wondering what the teacher wants. I glance back at Pari. Her expression flickers—hunger.

My chest is tight as I scoot as close to Mr. Eller as possible, hoping he'll keep his voice down. "What's up?"

"You looked a little lost in class again today, Ariel. Did you sign up for some tutoring?"

He's speaking softly, but there are so many people around. Someone could hear. "I've got a tutor," I say. "It's all good. Thanks." I turn before he can ask anything else and rush out of the room, hurrying down multiple hallways. Before I know it, I'm in front of the guidance office.

Ms. Hayes is smiling at something on her computer when I knock on her door. She glances up at me, eyes bright. "Morning, Ariel! Come look at this!"

Only one coffee cup on her desk today. My shoulders relax a bit. I sidle around the desk and look at her screen. It's a GIF of a basket of puppies that tipped over, and they're scrambling and running around the yard. "Adorable, right?" Ms. Hayes asks.

I grin, thinking of Ezekiel. My shift this weekend can't come soon enough. "Really cute," I agree.

She scrolls to the next GIF and asks, "To what do I owe the pleasure of your company this morning? Calculus going a bit better? I knew you could do it."

"Uh, yeah, well..." I scratch behind my ear. "I got a tutor."

"Excellent! Who?"

"Well, it didn't really work out, so I'm studying on my own again."

Her smile fades. "I'm sorry to hear that. What happened?"

"We, uh, didn't work well together."

"That's too bad," Ms. Hayes says. "Is there someone else you can reach out to for help?"

"Not really..." I run a hand through my hair. It's getting long, even with the curls. "Isn't there another option?"

"You can't drop the class. Students can't drop a math or science course."

"What? Drop a class?"

She stands and scans her corkboard, then yanks off a piece of blue paper and passes it to me. "October twenty-first. Here, you can keep that. It's the last day a student can withdraw from a course. You can't drop calculus, but you could drop another class to lighten your workload and make more time to study. An elective, like…" She types into her computer. "AP Spanish Literature."

"But I have an A in that class." I do, thanks to keeping up with the absurd amount of reading.

"I see that. Ariel, I'm only letting you know it's possible. But I agree. You should only drop a class if you have no other options. It will show up as a withdrawal on your record. Stick it out. I'm sure you can pull your grade up."

I stare down at the date. The two is smudged a bit, like the paper was pulled out of the printer too soon. September is almost over, so there's less than a month until the drop date.

I can't believe it's come to this. I still remember my first meeting with Ms. Hayes, when I was a freshman. At the time, I remember being excited. I was special. A smart kid. A *really* smart kid. She laid out my future in front of me like a journey of discovery and wonderful opportunities. Smaller classes. Better teachers. The perfect college applicant.

And the sick part is, when I'm doing well, I still feel like that special kid. Like I'm important for having so much work. Kids at school brag about all-nighters like badges of honor. There's this twisted part of me that feels proud, invigorated even, every time I stay up all night.

But I'm not special. I'm not smart enough. I put on a front, and now it's catching up to me.

"I didn't realize... It was just one grade..."

Ms. Hayes lowers her voice. "Look, I'm not supposed to share this, but I know Pari Shah is also applying early action to Harvard. If they only accept one student from here like last year, well, it's tight competition. You can't slip up."

Nausea sweeps over me.

"I'm not trying to overwhelm you, sweetie." Ms. Hayes reaches across the desk and pats my hand. "You have some decisions to make, that's all. I really think you should try again with that tutor. Will you do that for me?"

"Yeah." I slip my hand away, so she won't notice it shaking. "Sure. No problem."

———

"Want more?" Sook asks.

I nod, and she passes me the joint. It's down to the length of a pen cap, so when I take a hit, the smoke burns my eyes as much as my throat. "Another?" I ask, throwing the roach to the ground and grinding it out with the bottom of my metal water bottle. My head buzzes, fizzes.

"Fantastic idea," Sook replies.

We're sitting on a giant boulder, half a mile down the twisted trails of Tinder Hill. Canopies of leaves provide respite from the lingering summer heat, but the air is still tacky with humidity.

Sook pulls her lighter and a second joint from a floral-printed pencil pouch. She lights the joint and takes a hit before handing it to me.

The weed eases my racing pulse. I don't smoke often, especially not during the school year. Usually I like my express train of thoughts. It gives me an edge, helps me get more done. But for today, for the moment, I need to chill.

"Grateful Dead okay?" I ask, queuing up music on my phone.

Sook laughs. "Fine, I guess it is appropriate." She snatches the joint back from me. "Maybe it'll be good inspiration to mix it up anyways."

"Scarlet Begonias" begins to play. Sook and I finish the joint and lean back on the boulder. There's a cool breeze and a dappling of sun through the trees. Jerry Garcia's music mingles with the sound of wind ruffling leaves.

"Remember the first time we smoked?" Sook asks.

"Unfortunately, yes." I laugh. "Summer before ninth grade. Isaac had some, but he was worried they were going to drug test him for football, so he gave it to us."

"And we came right to this boulder," Sook says. "Well, after walking around for like two hours trying to find the least suspicious spot."

"And then we had to YouTube how to roll a joint. And how to light a joint. And how to smoke a joint."

Sook laughs. "It was a *lot* of work. Good thing we were fast learners."

I'll never forget that summer. My last months of freedom before high school; though I didn't know what high school would be like at the time. It was also the summer I started figuring out my sexuality.

I'd always been attracted to girls. My first kiss was as clichéd as it comes—a game of spin the bottle in sixth grade, a red-cheeked peck with Cindy Lao in front of twenty of our closest friends. Then in seventh grade, I had my first *real kiss*. It was Ava Newman's bat mitzvah party, and Hailey Bloom and I snuck out of the social hall and down to the east wing of the synagogue and made out for ten minutes in an empty preschool classroom. It was great.

But in eighth grade, I met Ian. He had blue eyes and played bass in orchestra, and my stomach flipped every time I saw him. I tried to brush off my interest as nothing, a silly infatuation. I liked girls, not guys. But the infatuation progressed into a hard-core crush, and one day, I was hanging out with him in the bass room after class, and he kissed me, and I kissed him back. And it was great, too.

It took a lot of processing. I knew bisexuality was a thing, but I guess I wanted it to be simple: straight or gay. Sook, already out as a lesbian, was the first person I confided in. Over that summer, she helped me confirm that yes, I am attracted to girls, and yes, I am attracted to guys, and yes, bisexuality is definitely a thing, and it might be complicated for some people to understand, but it'll get easier.

And then we watched that *Brooklyn Nine-Nine* scene where Rosa comes out as bisexual to the squad about a hundred times.

Sook nudges me. "Whatchya thinking about?"

I nudge back. "How much I love my best friend." I laugh. "God, I was such a dork back then. I tried so hard to *be high*. Like they are in the movies. I kept staring at my hands. And I decided I was ravenous, so I ate the leftover crusts in my lunch bag and acted like they were the best tasting things ever." I pause. "Damn, we should've brought snacks today."

"Ariel Stone doesn't have sour candy on him?"

"I've failed us. We'll never learn."

The song switches to "China Cat Sunflower."

"I like this one," Sook says.

"It's my favorite. Sounds like sunshine."

"I want to do that. Evoke a feeling so pure." Sook closes her eyes and hums, her fingers playing against her arm, like how I practice violin against mine.

As the song finishes, I ask, "So, are you going to tell me this special news of yours?"

Her smile is contagious. "I thought you'd never ask." She sits ups and straightens her shirt. "My parents offered me a deal."

I raise an eyebrow. "What kind of deal?"

"A deal that would let me pursue my music instead of going to their crap little school."

I clear my throat. "Okay, let's not call Dartmouth a *crap little school*."

Sook's parents are forcing her to go to Dartmouth, their alma mater, where she'll definitely be accepted thanks to their donations and Sook's intelligence. I try to muster sympathy for my best friend who *has* to go to an Ivy League school. I get that Sook doesn't want to go live in a small town, but an education at Dartmouth could set her up for life.

"Yeah, okay, I know," she says. "It's an amazing school. Great education. Etcetera. But it's like in the middle of nowhere. Not the place to rise to musical stardom. But if I go to school in Atlanta or even Athens, there's a huge music scene, and Malka and I can keep playing together."

"So what *is* this magical deal?" I ask.

"My parents say if Dizzy Daisies signs with an agent before graduation, I can pick whatever college I want!"

"Oh. Awesome."

Sook narrows her eyes. "Why aren't you more excited? Be more excited for me."

"I am!" I laugh and hold up my hands. "Promise. But how do you plan to *get* an agent?"

"With hard work and brilliance. Duh."

"All right, then." Sook is a determined person. If anyone can do it, then it's probably her. "Hey, speaking of brilliant female musicians, how are things going with your dream girl, lead Carousels' singer Clarissa?"

"Excellent!" she says. "We're mutuals on Tumblr now, *and* she listened to one of our songs and left the comment, 'Great sound.'"

"Impressive progress," I say, then fiddle with my phone, switching over to the Beatles. "Yesterday" begins to play. Gentle guitar fills the air. Sook and I pause for a moment, the lyrics washing over us.

"I wrote a new song," Sook says. "It could really use some violin."

"Sook—" I warn.

"Don't say no yet. Look, Malka is coming over for practice today. Join us and listen to the song. I'm only asking you to think about it." She nudges me and smiles, literally batting her eyelashes. "Please?"

I sigh, grinning despite myself. "*Fine*. But I'm not promising anything."

Sook squeals. "Deal!" Her eyes soften, and she leans into

me. "I'm glad we came out here today," she says. "We only have so many afternoons left together, you know?"

Her words hit harder than expected. A year from now, we'll likely live in different states and only see each other on school breaks. I've been so busy racing to the finish line, I haven't thought much about what happens when I cross it.

"We have plenty of afternoons left," I say. The music fades back in, with McCartney's melancholy voice and steady guitar. I wrap my arm around Sook and pull her into me. She's soft and warm and smells like yesterdays.

A baking sheet clatters to the floor. "I'm okay!" Sook yells. "We're good! The cookies are good!"

She giggles, and I snort, and then we both break into hysterical laughter.

"Oh my god," Malka says. "Are y'all high?"

"Yup," Sook responds.

Malka rolls her eyes. "Thanks for the invite."

"You were in class!" Sook says.

"Fair point, I suppose."

We're in Sook's Food Network–style kitchen. Gigantic island, marble countertops, stainless steel appliances, three ovens. We live in a well-off area, but Sook's family has some next-level money.

The kitchen smells like the inside of a warm cookie. Sook

is making my favorite: chocolate chip with chunks of melted caramel. I should be at home studying or at least practicing my violin solo, but it feels good to say *screw it* for an afternoon. Still, I can't relax entirely.

"We're home!" two voices call out. Her parents walk into the kitchen. "Mmm, smells good," her mom says, kissing Sook on the cheek. The female Dr. Kim has short hair and dresses like a teenager, preferring jeans and T-shirts over business attire. She's rarely home, always disappearing to work on her next invention. Most of their fortune comes from some kind of extra-strength fabric she sold to the military for an obscene sum.

"Ariel, it's good to see you!" Sook's dad says. "It's been a while." The male Dr. Kim prefers tailored slacks and expensive shirts. Maybe because he's a neurosurgeon he gets tired of spending most of his time in scrubs.

"Good to see you, too," I say. "Sook told me about the deal y'all made with her. Very cool of you."

"Ah, well," her mom says. "I'm sure she'll still end up at Dartmouth."

Sook's brow furrows. "I'm *going* to get an agent."

Her mom nods with a soft smile. "Your music is very good, sweetheart. But you have your entire life to play it. I don't want you stressing yourself out too much."

"And you'll love it at Dartmouth, Sook. You can play music there!" her dad says.

Sook mutters something under her breath about shitty coffeehouse open mics and turns back to taking the cookies off the tray. We keep chatting as her parents put the groceries away. Then we grab the cooling cookies. I pile four on my napkin while biting into a fifth. The caramel is warm and chewy. Bless these cookies.

We thud downstairs to Sook's basement. There are soundproof walls, an array of instruments, and leather couches. Sook settles at the table with the Mac desktop, while Malka and I jump on the leather couch.

"Give me a second, guys," Sook says. "I want to add a couple of practices to the calendar."

Malka groans. "More practices? You already added an extra each week."

Sook points upstairs. "Those people need to learn to take me seriously. We're going to get an agent and shock the hell out of them. No Dartmouth for me."

Malka bites back a sigh and turns to me. "We love her, right?"

"We do." I nod. "We do love her."

"I heard that," Sook says, typing at the computer.

"Good!" Malka shouts.

I pick at a thread on the pillow I'm holding. "So what's going on with you?" I ask. "How's college?"

Malka shrugs. "All right, I guess." She glances around, then clears her throat. "I don't know, I'm trying to…I don't know."

I nudge her. "Trying to what? What's going on?"

"Nothing." She waves her hand. "Never mind."

I eye her.

"Really!" she says. "Hey, did you know there's a Chabad on campus? I think I'm going to check out an event. Free food. Jews. Should be fun, right?"

"Can't go wrong with free food and Jews," I agree.

"Okay!" Sook says. "And done! Check your email. I sent the new calendar."

Malka pulls out her phone and sighs. "Really, Sook? Three practices a week? That might be difficult for me."

"It'll be fine," Sook says.

"No. My dorm isn't exactly down the street. That's a lot of driving. And you know traffic is a nightmare."

"But you're here literally every weekend. So that's two of the practices right there," Sook responds. She doesn't get it. She doesn't understand when everything doesn't work like she plans it.

"Yeah…" Malka says. "But I don't always hang around Sunday, and I have shul, and homework, and a life."

"Dude," Sook says. "You're never at college. I'm sure you have the time."

Malka stiffens. I'm about to defuse the situation, when she clears her throat and says, "C'mon, let's play the new song for Ariel."

"Okay!" Sook's clueless she just bulldozed her friend. I should talk to her later. It's a best friend's duty to call each other out about shitty behavior.

They walk over to their equipment. It's only a two-girl band, so Malka plays guitar, and Sook plays piano, sings, and records their drum tracks. I slip out my Kindle and continue reading *Crime and Punishment* while they tune their instruments and warm up.

But I can't focus. My thoughts drift to Amir. I messed up. I should apologize because he deserves an apology—and also because I need his help if I want any chance of passing this calculus test.

"Ready!" Sook says.

As they begin to play, I send off a text before I can overthink it: *Sorry about yesterday. Are you free again tonight? I'd like to give tutoring another shot if you're open to it...*

I turn over my phone and scoot it far away on the couch, too nervous to look at it. I'll check it when the song is over.

Sook presses a button on the keyboard, and the drums fill out the song. Their sound is different than my usual classic rock soundtrack, but it's catchy and relaxed. Sook's fingers run across the keyboard in a comfortable rhythm, and then Malka joins in on guitar. Sook's voice is sweet but has this little growl when you're least expecting it, drawing you in again and again.

It's short and entrancing. And I can hear exactly where a

violin melody would add to its depth. As the song finishes, both girls grin, and I applaud. The ghost of the melody still plays in my head. "That was great," I say. "Loved it."

"It'd sound even better with strings," Sook replies.

"It would," I agree. "But I can't."

"C'mon," Sook says. "Just for a couple songs."

"Sook…"

"You don't have to commit forever! If it sounds good, we can always find another violinist down the road. Please, Ariel. I think this could really help us get an agent. A couple songs. C'mon."

Sook stares me down, eyes pleading. I know how badly she wants this. And it would be fun to play with them. And maybe if it goes well, I can even include it on my college application. This could be the passion I'm lacking.

"Please," she says.

I pinch the bridge of my nose. "Okay. Fine."

"Really?" Malka asks, eyebrow raised.

I shrug. "Yep. Really."

"Ah! Yes!" Sook squeals. "You're the best. Truly the best. I love you."

"Mm-hmm," I say. "Love you too."

Sook and Malka launch into another song that could use some violin. I stare at my phone, nervous. Then I turn it over quick, like ripping off a Band-Aid. No response from Amir.

My stomach drops. But then, as I'm about to put the phone

back down, a text comes in. Amir: *I think you can apologize better than that*

I quickly text back: *Will you let me apologize in person? Is your family home? I can bring textbooks and snacks*

My heart thumps as I wait for an answer, watching the three gray dots start and stop. Finally: *Empty house for the next couple hours. If you bring Publix Bakery sugar cookies, I'll let you in*

I grin and text back: *Done and done*

SIX

"I should never eat sweets again," I say.

Then I pick up a second sugar cookie and bite into it.

"I must give Sook credit," Amir says, pulling apart one of her cookies and popping a piece in his mouth. "These are incredible. *Almost* as good as Publix."

I snagged some extra cookies from Sook's house and then ran to Publix to buy sugar cookies and chocolate milk. When Amir opened the door, he peered into the bag like he didn't trust I'd brought the goods, then nodded and said, "You may come in."

"So." Amir picks up a sugar cookie next and nibbles on it. My eyes flicker to his lips, and the back of my neck burns. "What happened yesterday? I thought we were working well together. And then, well, you were kind of rude."

"Yeah." I nod. "I, uh…"

"If something's going on, you can talk to me."

His unguarded gaze fixes on me, and I feel like I'm under a hundred spotlights. How does Amir know something is up when my own parents and best friend don't suspect a thing? Maybe when you aren't as close with someone, they have the distance to see you clearly.

Amir watches me, not with pressure, but patience. Still, my pulse races. I pick up my napkin and shred a corner of it. "Yeah, well it's…"

No lie comes.

Maybe that's a good thing.

"Um, the truth is—" I take a short breath, my left leg shaking up and down. I'm too wound up, shoulders too tense, heartbeat too fast. It's like I physically can't keep this all to myself.

So I meet Amir's eyes. They're dark and warm, and they steady me. "If I fail calculus, I won't be valedictorian."

Amir waits. He knows there's more.

I keep shredding the napkin. "And worse than that, Harvard might find out. Why would Harvard accept someone failing—" Harvard. I could be rejected from Harvard. Years of stress and sleep deprivation for nothing. I suddenly feel ill from the sugar coursing through my system. "I've spent years working toward this one goal. It's all I am. I'm not Ariel, the one with the band, or Ariel, the one with the camera.

I'm Ariel, the one with the highest GPA. That's it." My voice cracks with the next words. "If I don't have perfect grades, then who am I?"

Amir's eyes flicker with sympathy, and I can tell whatever he says next will be too much for me, so I continue, "I'm sorry I snapped yesterday. Really. I shouldn't have put any of this on you. It's my own crap to deal with. And I know other people have real problems, like affording college, or even affording college applications. I'm just feeling sorry for myself."

I take a short breath. Okay, Ariel. Enough talking.

"Hmm," Amir says. He studies his spiral notebook, hands clasped in front of him. After a moment, he nods and looks up. My shoulders relax when our eyes connect. The sympathy is mostly gone, though I'm nervous he'll want to pry further. "You know, people do have more difficult problems. But your anxieties are still real. They still count, yeah?"

A catch forms in my throat. "*Yeah*."

"Do you want to talk about it more?" Amir asks.

I draw lines in my notebook, scratching until my pencil almost rips through the page. "Maybe we can just study?" I ask. "If that's okay."

"Sure."

I nod and meet his gaze again. "Thanks, Amir."

"Hey." He smiles. "Thanks for the cookies."

_____

Two hours later, I'm leading us through my fifth consecutive problem when Amir says, "Crap."

My pencil pauses. "What'd I do wrong?"

"No, not you. We're out of practice problems. I should've gotten us some additional material."

"I can find some for next time," I offer.

Amir raises an eyebrow. "Next time?"

"Oh, I meant…if you don't mind… Or, if you have time. You know, to study again. Is that okay?"

When he laughs, it lights up his whole face. "I never thought I'd see a nervous Ariel Stone. It's really messing with my head."

"Really?" I lean forward. "How do I normally seem?"

"Sure of yourself," Amir says. "Scattered, but sure of yourself. You're always doing five things at once but seem on top of it all."

"So I've done it? I've mastered the look of having my shit together?"

"I'd say so. It's a bit like watching a stampede. Ordered chaos." His eyes are bright. "How do you see me? I'm curious."

He's close enough I can smell the spearmint and basil. My pulse thuds fast. "Well, you're usually quiet, paying more attention to your camera than the people around you. And sometimes you can seem a little…" I cough out the next words. "…*into yourself*."

He laughs, loud, then leans back in his chair and scratches the stubble on his jaw. "Perhaps I am, a little bit," he says.

"Though to be fair, all my self-confidence is mixed with intense self-doubt. Like my friends—"

"Your cool, older friends?" I interject.

He laughs again. "Yeah, them. They're all older than me. And sometimes I catch myself trying to impress them, as if I have to make up for the fact that I'm younger."

"Why *do* you hang out with older people?"

He shrugs. "I have some friends at school, but I don't know. It happened naturally. I connected with Rasha's classmates, and over time, I met friends of friends and so on, and they became my circle." He pauses. "I like the excuse to get out of the house, create some distance. I love my family, but they can be overwhelming. It's hard to get a word in when they're all talking at once. Sometimes I need to get away, decompress."

His family is like mine—loud.

For an introspective person like Amir, it must be a lot to deal with. Which frustrates me a little because it means, for years, I've been missing out on this guy sitting right next to me.

"Well, I'm glad I get full sentences from you now," I say.

He laughs. "Thanks. So, wait, what were we talking about?"

"Um, studying together again."

"Right! Yes, let's do it. This material is difficult for me also."

"Please," I say. "You're like a math savant."

His eyes tease me. "Perhaps compared to you."

"Not cool."

"Kidding." He grins. "Well, mostly. Let's finish this problem. You got it?"

"We'll see."

His grin widens. "You've got it."

I work through the steps, hesitating before punching numbers in the calculator, running back over all my handwork. My pencil wavers over the page. I'm about to ask Amir for help when he says, "Keep going."

His assurance steadies me. I nod, take a short breath, and finish the problem. I glance at Amir afterward, unsure. "Is it right?"

"Let's see." He flips to the back of the book, then looks at my page, then back at his book.

"Well?"

He nods. "It looks like we might have two math savants in the room."

"Awesome." Suddenly, I feel lighter. I stand and bounce on my heels a couple of times. I want to punch the air like that guy at the end of *The Breakfast Club*, but that might be a bit much.

"You okay?" Amir asks.

"Very okay. I think I'm actually going to pass that test on Friday."

"You'll do better than pass. I'll be both pissed and proud when you get a higher grade than me."

I laugh, then walk over to their fridge. For the first time since failing that quiz, I feel truly happy, almost buoyant. Amir is right—I will do better than pass. I'll bring up my grade, and everything will be as it should be again. "Mind if I grab something to eat? I'm starving. All sugar, no substance."

"Sure. I'm hungry, too. I should eat before I head out."

"Head out?" I glance at my phone. "It's almost nine."

"My friend Jacob has a showing at Elaine's. It's this great gallery downtown—small, but Elaine always tracks down the best artists. It'd be incredible to see my work there one day. Anyway, I promised him I'd stop by."

I scratch behind my ear. "Does, uh, Jacob go to our school, or is he an older friend?"

"Older friend. He's, like, twenty-two, I think."

Twenty-two. That's too old for them to be a thing, right? Still, my positivity trickles away. Whether he's trying to be cool or not, Amir hangs out at art galleries on weeknights with interesting, older friends. I try to shake the feeling of rejection. Only days ago, I didn't have a spare thought for Amir. But now, I'm having trouble keeping my eyes or thoughts off him.

I'm sure it's nothing. He's the first person I opened up to about my school stress. There's a relief being around him. That's all.

He glances at me and smiles. My cheeks heat.

Yep, I'm sure it's nothing.

Ten minutes later, we've cooked up a double batch of ramen noodles and munched on an entire bag of sour watermelon pieces while it cooked because why not have more sugar?

"Glad to know you're a great chef like me," Amir says, divvying up the ramen.

"Who has time to learn how to cook?"

"I wish I could." We head to the table with the ramen and a bowl of cut fruit. "I'm hungry all the time, and my parents unfortunately have jobs other than feeding me. It'd be fantastic if I could whip up some biryani whenever I want it."

"True, if I could cook matzo ball soup, I'd probably have it every day."

"I've never tried it."

I put down my spoon and gape at Amir. "You've never had matzo ball soup?"

Amir sips his ramen, looking unconcerned. "Nope."

I angle my chair toward him and lean forward, hands braced on my knees. "But, dude, you're missing out on the best food in the world."

He laughs. "You're intense about this soup."

"It's a soup worthy of intensity. Seriously, though, y'all have come for dinner so many times. We've never had matzo ball soup?"

"Nope. But your mom did make brisket once, and it was unspeakably good."

"Mmm, love brisket." I sip my ramen broth. Delicious sodium. "I can't believe you haven't had the soup, though. You're going to have to come over. I'll ask Mom to make it soon."

"Sure." He grins at me. "Sounds like a plan."

A new voice cuts in. "Ariel? Hey! What are you doing here?"

Amir and I both look up to find Rasha in the doorway. She's wearing all black, from her hijab to her motorcycle boots. I guess we were talking too much to hear her walk in. It's still so strange spending time with *chatty Amir*.

"Oh, hey," I say, shifting in my seat. Damn. I wanted to be gone by the time anyone got home. "Um, I was…"

"He was helping me study for calc," Amir says, pointing to the textbooks.

The lie fills me with both guilt and relief. "Really?" Rasha asks. "I didn't know you two…hung out."

"Yeah, sometimes," I say. "Want some ramen?" I ask, eager for a subject change.

Rasha makes a face. "Gross. I will take some of that fruit, though." She sits, kicks her feet up on the edge of the table, and picks out a piece of cantaloupe. "Class went on *forever* today. It should be illegal for a three-hour lecture to run long, I'm just saying."

"Sounds rough," I respond.

Still, I'm jealous. In less than a year, I'll be the one in

college. Giant lecture halls with a hundred people in the class, no one focusing on me, on my grades. No pressure to be the best, only to be good enough.

"Anyways," Rasha continues. "Now I'm behind on homework. And I was supposed to hand out fliers for the mosque's Halal Food Festival today, so I guess I'll have to do that in the morning. Amir, you're going, right? You promised!"

"Uh, sure," Amir says. Rasha has always been more religiously observant than the rest of her family. She tries to get her parents to go to services with her, like how Malka urges her parents to join her at shul.

"And," she continues, "I have all of this stuff to do for *Our Campus*. This administration gives us no rest. We're doing a politics segment every week now."

"*Our Campus*?" I ask, glancing at Amir.

He nods. "It's this—"

"It's the podcast I work on!" Rasha jumps in. "There are a few at our school, but *Our Campus* is the largest. I scored an internship freshman year, and because I'm a badass, I'm already an assistant producer. We broadcast all kinds of stuff: politics, arts, personal stories, music, and obviously some segments about the school. It's awesome. I want to get this brother of mine on to talk about his photography. I think it could really jump-start his brand, but he keeps refusing."

"I don't want a brand, Rasha," Amir mutters.

"Well, if you want to have any success in photography, you'd better get started on one."

"I'm not looking for—" Amir tenses, but his voice stays calm. "I'll keep it in mind."

"That's all I'm saying! I'm only trying to help. I love you." She stands and kisses the top of his head. "Anyways." Rasha turns back to me. "We produce all sorts of segments."

Amir looks like he wants to say something else, but then picks up his phone and zones out. Rasha is a little intense, but she's only trying to help.

As I digest what Rasha said, something clicks. "So, music," I say. "Do you guys have bands on the show?"

"Yeah, all the time!"

"Are y'all open for auditions?"

She pops a grape into her mouth and chews, then leans forward, eyes bright. "Wait, are you in a band? How did I not know this? Amir!" She looks at him as if it's his fault somehow, and he shrugs. "Why didn't you tell me, dude?"

He's still on his phone. I think he's on Tumblr. I spy a GIF of Hermione punching Malfoy.

"I just joined one," I tell Rasha. "Dizzy Daisies. You know my friend Sook? You've met at my house, I'm sure. Oh, and Malka! She's a freshman now at your college."

"Malka Rothberg! Love that girl. I've seen her on campus a few times. I forgot they had a band." She nods, excited. "Yeah,

I think I listened to them a year ago. They were pretty great. They're still together? You joined them?"

"Yeah, they needed some violin, so I'm going to play with them a bit."

"That's awesome. We only feature students of the school, but as long as one of them is in the band, you're good to go. Oh my god, let's set this up! Such a great idea."

"Really? Cool." I smile. "I'll give you their info so you guys can coordinate."

"I can't wait to pitch this. Maybe they'll even let me produce it!"

Twenty minutes later, Rasha excuses herself with a squeal, saying she's got to shower. I pack my bag as she leaves. Sook will be psyched. This kind of exposure could help them get an agent.

"So…" I say. My bag is packed, and Amir is still looking at his phone. "I'm gonna head out. I'm sorry Rasha doesn't get the photography thing."

Amir gives the world's tiniest shrug. "It's fine."

I bite back a suggestion. I'm sure he knows how to handle his family best, and it's not my place to step in. "Okay, have fun at your show."

"Thanks." He doesn't look up. I pick at my nail. Maybe those feelings were a figment of my imagination, or a side effect of learning calculus.

I grab my bag, then pause. "I think you'll make an awesome doctor."

This time he looks up, a smile warming his eyes. "Thanks, Ariel."

"No problem." My grin is too wide, but I can't help it.

Oy gevalt.

SEVEN

"I love this class," Pari whispers as she passes me the popcorn.

I grab a handful and offer her some of my candy. "Sour gummy worms?"

"Yes, please!"

Our teacher Mrs. Chen is playing an episode of *West Wing* for class today, and we were all allowed to bring snacks. AP Gov is always a welcome stress relief to wind down the day.

My phone buzzes. It's another excitement GIF from Sook. I told her Rasha wants the band on the podcast, and she is beyond thrilled. *Best best friend ever*, she typed with a string of emojis.

Mrs. Chen sits at her desk grading papers while we watch. If only all my classes could be like this. Reasonable workload. Straightforward assignments. TV in class.

"This semester is dragging by, isn't it?" Pari asks. "Can't we graduate already?"

"Yeah," I say. Really, time is slipping away too quickly. My Harvard application is due November first, and I still haven't started it. "Have you started your apps yet?"

She picks at her chipped purple polish. "Yeah, I already sent a bunch off."

I swallow a piece of popcorn too fast. It sticks in my throat, and I cough loud enough the guys in front of me glance back.

"Here," Pari says, passing her water.

I unscrew the cap and sip. "Thanks." Another sip. "So you already got yours in?"

Logically, I know colleges don't weigh early applications any more favorably than those sent in a day before the deadline.

Less logically, I'm freaked out. What if Harvard falls in love with Pari before they even get a chance to meet me?

"I still have a few left because I can't apply early every-where. But most of them are done. They took *forever*." She grabs the water from me and takes a sip. "I kind of panicked last year when you, well, you know, with the computer science course. It was hard dealing with that, knowing I wouldn't be valedictorian. So I figured it was best to get those applications in and be done with it. I keep telling myself I can relax now, but I guess it's not actually going to happen until I'm walking across that stage."

She pauses. "There aren't many people who get what we're going through. I mean, Isaac works hard, but it's different."

I nod, shoulders tense. "Yeah."

There was a time when we were all in this together. As freshman, there was only one AP class we could take. I remember we felt like the cool kids—important because we had extra work. There were, like, a hundred of us taking the class, and on weekends a dozen of us would meet up at Whole Foods. We'd make a big deal of it, pushing tables together and spreading out all our textbooks and papers, but then we'd mess around talking and eating all afternoon.

But the more AP classes I took, the smaller that peer group became, and the less time I had to pretend to study because there was so much actual work to get done.

I want to open up to Pari, but part of me wonders if she's trying to get me to put my guard down. Maybe she knows about the failed quiz and wants me to slip further.

Like she said, I won't relax until I'm across that stage.

Laughing classmates draw our attention back to *West Wing*. Pari giggles. "I love this show. It's my favorite binge."

"I've only seen a couple episodes," I say, grateful for the subject change. "Maybe I'll watch it next year."

Pari's expression shifts. She gives me this kind smile. "Almost done, Ariel." She sighs and rests her head on her arms, staring at the screen. "We're almost done."

I wave at Janet as I drive into the Jewish Community Center parking lot. She smiles and steps out of the security booth, taking my license and checking the picture. Protocol demands it even though she's known me since I was a little kid. "Nice to see you, Ariel."

"You too! How are you?"

"Oh, you know, pretty good. Glad those hot days seem to be behind us."

She waves me forward, and I pull into the giant lot, driving around to get to the soccer fields in the back corner. Usually Rachel gets a ride home with her friend's mom, but the friend is home sick today. I park and climb out of the car.

It's a shockingly nice day. Cool with the right amount of sun warming my skin. I stretch my arms into the air and yawn, closing my eyes, enjoying the slight breeze. I'm early, so I put in my headphones, and play Simon & Garfunkel. Their familiar voices comfort me.

I should study or at least turn on my *Crime and Punishment* audiobook, but it's only a few minutes. I can let myself relax for a few minutes. Sometimes, I go running with Dad's ancient iPod instead of my phone because it forces me to empty my mind, do nothing but listen to music.

I close my eyes and lean against the hood of my car as "The Boxer" plays. I must nod off because my buzzing phone stirs me. I glance down.

It's Amir: *What are you listening to?*

I look up, to my right and then my left. Amir is leaning against a large tree overlooking the soccer field.

I bite my lip.

He waves and gives me a half smile, which for whatever reason is infinitely more stomach fluttering than a full smile. I grin, too wide and telling, then rub my hands against my jeans, trying to flex out my sudden nerves. The sun shines on him, revealing light streaks in his dark hair.

I walk over, and for a moment, I stand in comfortable silence at his side, inhaling his scent of spearmint and basil. My shoulder is only an inch from his. If I shifted my feet, our arms would brush together. From up here, we can see the entire soccer field. The girls are finishing up practice, drilling field goals, one after another. The familiar sound of the thwack of the ball carries up to us on the hill and stirs something in me. I miss it, the focus, the exhilaration of concentrating on nothing but the game.

Amir sighs and closes his eyes. I stare, shameless, taking in the stubble around his jaw, the slope of his nose, the curve of his lips.

He shifts toward me and cracks his eyes open. They're golden brown in the sun. "It's a beautiful day, isn't it? Perfect quidditch weather."

I raise an eyebrow and fail to tamp down a laugh. "Quidditch weather?"

"It's a real sport! National leagues and everything."

"Nerd," I say.

He grins. "I know. But seriously, I want to join a team in college."

"I'm a little intrigued."

"I'll show you videos of matches later, I promise, when it's not so nice out." He exhales a slow breath. "I wish we could have this weather forever."

"Fall is the best season. It's a fact. So, I guess you're getting Sara from practice?"

"I am. You're getting Rachel?"

"Yup."

We enjoy the silence for a bit longer, but then Amir says, "Calc test tomorrow."

I stiffen, but then smirk as I say, "You trying to ruin this nice day?"

"You're ready. I know you are."

It's true our last study session together went well, and I've been acing all the practice problems at home, but still, if I don't pass tomorrow, if I don't get an A tomorrow…

I grip the car keys in my hand, the metal teeth pressing into my skin.

"You're ready," Amir repeats. I look at him. His gaze is steady, assured. "Ariel, I promise you're ready."

I nod and breathe out, releasing my grip on the keys.

Singing erupts from the field. The girls are skipping around and laughing. "I think practice is over," I say.

Amir nods. "Looks like it."

"I should probably get Rachel home. Study some more."

"Eh," Amir says.

He leans back against the tree, and so do I, and this time our arms brush together.

It is a beautiful day.

I read the test instructions twice.

Okay. I can do this. Right? I can do this.

It's Friday morning, and the clock is ticking as everyone concentrates on their tests.

Okay, focus. Write out the steps.

I tackle the first problem. Easy. Almost too easy. I check my work. It's correct. Then I check it again. Still correct.

I take my time with the rest of the test, glancing back and forth a dozen times to make sure I input the right numbers into my calculator and triple-checking my work. As I flip to the final page, Pari gets up to turn in her paper. Then more students, one after another. When Amir gets back to his desk, he pulls out the third Harry Potter book, a well-worn paperback. I laugh, quick and soft, but he hears and glances at me. "Nerd," I whisper, pointing to the book.

He grins.

I turn back to my test, stomach tightening. Right. Still have to finish this.

I gnaw a sliver of a hangnail. At least I'm in the back of the room. Maybe no one will notice I'm the last one with the test. I glance at the clock. Shit, only ten minutes left. I need to concentrate. If people notice, then so be it. Today, a perfect grade is more important than anything else.

I get through the final problems and check my work once more. Then I walk up with my paper.

Mr. Eller looks at me. He speaks in a brusque tone. "Wait here, Ariel."

I shift on my feet, feeling the eyes of my classmates. Mr. Eller pulls out a red pen, and I take a sharp breath. Is he torturing me on purpose? Grading mine right here? He slides an answer sheet out of a folder, and before I know it, his pen is running down my test. My heart thumps. I feel ill. Checkmark, checkmark, checkmark.

I'm unsteady as the pages flip by. Checkmark, checkmark, checkmark.

He gets to the final problem, looks up at me, nods, and checks it off, too. "Well done, Ariel. Perfect score."

Adrenaline courses through me. I did it. A perfect score. The relief makes my head swim. But I'm still too aware of the people around me to celebrate. So I say "Thanks" and head back to my desk.

As I go to sit, my eyes lock with Amir's.

Well? he seems to ask.

I give him a thumbs-up.

He shakes his head and whispers, "*Dork.*"

When the bell rings, I go to tell Amir just how well I did, but he hurries from the classroom, not even glancing at me.

Oh.

I thought maybe…

I don't know what I thought.

Isaac tosses his squeeze ball into the air and catches it. "What'd Mr. Eller want?"

"To grade my test in front of me. No clue why." I shrug my shoulders, then casually add, "I got a perfect score, so…"

"You two," Isaac says, pointing at Pari and me, "are way too smart. Stop making the rest of us look bad."

"Dude," Pari says. "You have a 3.98 weighted GPA. I think you're doing okay."

"By national standards sure, but by Etta Fields High School standards, I'm barely holding on to the top ten percentile. This school is ridiculous."

"It's not that bad," I respond, though I'm not sure why I'm defending this place. Maybe I have Stockholm syndrome.

"Not that bad?" Isaac asks. "When we're losing a football

game, our fans chant *SAT scores*, because at least we're always beating the other school academically. C'mon. That's ridiculous. I hope colleges know what this place is like and don't focus on rankings too much. They shouldn't even put the rank on transcripts at a school like ours. I swear if I don't get into Vanderbilt..."

It's hard to believe Isaac is worried about Vanderbilt. He's the perfect college applicant. Varsity football player and a load of AP classes. Colleges will probably fall over themselves to accept him. Pari rubs circles on his back. "You'll be fine," she says. "I'm sure you'll get in. You have to because that campus was awesome, and I want to be able to visit you."

"Yeah, man," I say. "You're a great student."

"Yeah, well, I don't only need to get in. I need a good scholarship. Not all of us can—" He hesitates.

"What?" Pari asks.

He shakes his head. "Look, I know getting into an Ivy is the first priority for you guys, but some of us have to get into school *and also* be able to afford tuition. *Great* isn't always enough for scholarships. Hopefully all these freaking AP classes will help."

I hesitate, then say, "That's rough. But you're doing everything you can. Don't stress." *And the hypocrite of the year award goes to.* "I'm gonna grab a Coke before class. I'll see y'all later."

I head down the hallway, feeling weirdly low despite my perfect score, but then hear someone call my name: "Ariel!"

I turn. Amir. He's standing alone at the end of the hall by an emergency exit and a single back bay of lockers. I walk toward him, twisting one of my backpack straps around my hand.

"Sorry I ran out of class," he says. "My doctor called. I've been trying to schedule a check-up for a week."

I groan. "Mom makes me set my appointments now, too. Grown-up responsibilities are the worst."

"Agreed. So? The test. You seemed happy. How'd you do?"

I sweep hair off my forehead. "Oh, you know…perfect score. No big deal."

"Really?"

I smile. "Yeah, really."

"Hell yeah, Ariel!" He high-fives me. Our hands clasp and stay intertwined for a moment too long, then two moments too long. His eyes spark. The touch overwhelms me. I need to do something with the electricity buzzing through my system.

I *want* to do something with it.

But then the first bell rings.

Amir glances up at the hall clock, and his hand slips from mine.

"We should probably go to class," I say.

"Yeah, probably."

We're both still smiling.

"I feel like I just aced my O.W.L.s," I say.

His eyes widen. "Oh my god, excellent Harry Potter reference."

113

"I'm learning from the best."

"Come for the calculus, stay for the Potter trivia."

"That should be your slogan when you start tutoring professionally." I clear my throat. "Thank you. If I haven't said that yet."

"It was my pleasure."

The word *pleasure* rolls smoothly from his lips.

I pause. "Why did you agree to help me?"

"You asked," he says, like it's the most obvious thing in the world. He takes a half a step forward, and I swallow hard, pulse racing.

The second bell rings.

Amir leans back and scratches his jaw.

"So, to class, I guess," I say.

"Yep. To class."

I bite my lip. Amir's gaze moves to it. He shakes his head with a slight grin. "I'll see you later, Ariel."

Yes, he will.

"Saul, come see this," Mom says. "I think our son is possessed."

I roll my eyes. "Really?"

The microwave beeps, and I take out the now defrosted ground beef. A pot of water boils on the stove, waiting for pasta, and there's chopped onion and broccoli on the counter.

"You're cooking," she says.

Dad appears in the doorway. "He's cooking, Miriam."

Mom looks at him. "Is this a fever dream?"

"I cook sometimes," I say. Though I'm not exactly sure what to do with the ground beef now. Do I put it in the pan? Or am I supposed to put oil down first?

Mom laughs. "I'll take that." She grabs the ground beef from me. "Come watch."

As I observe, Dad finishes the rest of the chopping and pulls out another pan for the vegetables. He puts in a splash of olive oil and minced garlic, and soon the kitchen smells delicious. "What's gotten into you?" Dad asks. "Good day?"

Excellent day. I passed my test.

I passed my test, and Amir…

Heat rises to my cheeks. I clear my throat. "Yeah, pretty good. I'm going into the city tonight for that Dizzy Daisies podcast taping. And I had free time after school, so I thought I'd cook, and we could have an early Shabbat dinner first."

Free time. The concept is so foreign that when I got home this afternoon, I stared at the TV for ten minutes—without actually turning it on. I stared at the blank screen and tried to compute what one actually does with their time when they don't have piles of homework.

Today, I aced my calculus test, took my *Crime and Punishment* essay test, and turned in a paper for AP Spanish Lit. It's a Friday afternoon, and since Rosh Hashanah services are on Monday and Tuesday, four days with zero school stretch before me. I have to practice the *Scheherazade* solo, and I have work for some other classes, but four days is more than enough time to get it all done.

So I stared at the TV until my stomach grumbled, and I realized: *Oh, people cook in their free time!*

My parents have been cooking for me for almost eighteen years. It'd be nice to return the favor. "Bow ties or penne?" I ask, grabbing pasta from the cabinet.

"Hmm…" Mom says.

"Bow ties!" Rachel shouts, skipping into the kitchen and then racing around the counter.

"Easy there!" Mom says. "You have too much energy. I can't believe they got rid of fifth-grade recess at that school of yours. C'mon." She passes Rachel a spatula. "Help me season the meat."

Twenty minutes later, dinner is ready, and the prayers have been said, and we're all settled around the table, digging into steaming plates of pasta and meat sauce.

"Mmm," Rachel says. "Who seasoned this? It's delicious."

We all laugh.

"Thank you for dinner, Ariel," Dad says.

"I had some help."

"But it's the thought that counts." Dad takes a bite of garlic bread. "Mmm, and you're the one who thought to defrost this bread, so the thought counts for a lot."

"Watch this!" Rachel tosses a piece high in the air and catches it in her mouth. She smiles while chewing.

"Nice." I grin, leaning back as Mom starts us off on bloopers and highlights.

I'm so ready for high school to be over, but next year, I won't be here for weekly Shabbat dinner. I'll likely only have a few breaks a year. I'm ready to graduate, but as I look around the table and listen to my family talk about their week, I can't help but wish moving away didn't mean moving away from them.

EIGHT

"How large is your audience?" Sook asks. She trails around the recording studio and inspects the equipment, a journal and pen in hand.

"Depends on the week," Rasha answers, fiddling with the microphone, screwing it left then right. I've never seen Rasha nervous. Maybe it has something to do with that girl Lois, one of the podcast's executive producers, not-at-all-subtly watching us from her office. This is the first episode Rasha is producing alone, and it looks like someone isn't ready to give up control. "There we go!" Her voice brightens as the microphone clicks into place.

"Do you need any help?" Malka offers. We're sitting on an extra table pressed against the back wall of the room. Malka mentioned Rasha invited her to observe a recording earlier this week, so this is her second time here.

"Yeah, need help?" I ask.

"I'm good. Thank you, though!" Rasha is wearing nice jeans and a blazer. She looks like a producer. "We'll be ready soon. Sook, I'm not sure of our exact audience size, but we have the most downloads of any campus podcast. And we're in the top hundred for the Atlanta area."

Sook draws her pen down the page. "And you'll link to our social media pages in the show notes, right? Oh! And does your Twitter post when a new episode is up? Will you tag the handle for our band? Crap, I need to update our page." She scribbles something down. "And how much of an increase in web traffic do your guests experience?"

Rasha gives us an is-she-for-real look, and I shake my head and grin. Sook, oblivious, flips a page in her notebook and keeps writing. "I'm really not in charge of that stuff," Rasha answers. "I can put you in touch with someone on the business side if you want."

Sook already has out her phone. "Fantastic. What's their number?"

I bite back a laugh. Malka snorts.

"Okay," Rasha says. "We're all set up! Sook, I'll get you that information afterward. Ariel, if it's all right with you, I'd love to interview Malka and Sook first, and then we'll bring you in at the end."

"You don't have to," I say. "We haven't even had a practice together yet."

"We'll only do a few minutes," Rasha replies. "That okay?"

I shrug. "Sure." I guess it'll make my "music career" searchable if I decide to write about Dizzy Daisies for my essay.

The girls settle around the circular table with the microphone in the middle. I ease back, leaning on my hands. Rasha counts them down and begins, welcoming everyone to the show. Her recording voice is slightly different, richer, and she takes time with pronunciation, giving space to each syllable.

She eases in with basic questions. When the band started—seventh grade. Where they practice—Sook's basement. What instruments they play—Malka guitar and Sook vocals, keys, drums, and whatever synthesized sounds they want.

But as the questions become more complex, I notice Sook tense up. She spins a gold ring on her index finger and takes long pauses before answering, like each word has to be perfect.

Malka keeps the flow better. Her conversation with Rasha sounds natural, like they're hanging out. They go back and forth for a few minutes about what brought Malka to the band in the first place. And then Rasha asks, "Malka, did you think about leaving the band when you graduated from high school?"

"No," Malka answers. "The commute can be tough, but I love Sook. She's talented and knows what she wants. Sook is going places, and at least for now, I want to tag along."

Sook blinks, like it takes a second to comprehend the compliment. It seems to unwind some of that tension she's holding. She leans over and kisses Malka on the cheek, then says, "Malka forgot to mention she's also incredibly talented. I'm lucky she stayed with me, and I feel confident we can go far together. If we dedicate ourselves and keep at it, we'll make it."

The conversation relaxes again, as they tell a story of their first gig, which was a total nightmare and somehow involved a clown. Laughing, I glance up at the window, expecting to find Lois glaring at us, but instead, my eyes lock with Amir. He smiles and gives a little wave.

I mouth *hi*, then feel ridiculous.

Amir's gaze switches to the girls. It seems like he's listening to them record. Maybe there's a speaker outside this room. I wonder what he's doing here. Visiting his sister?

Rasha calls to get my attention, "Ariel, come join us." I jolt, then clear my throat and stand, suddenly nervous. I walk over and join them at the table.

"Ariel is also a high school senior," she says into the mic. "He's joining this duo to play violin for some of their songs. Ariel, what drew you to Dizzy Daisies?"

My mind goes blank. I don't know the answer. I'm not prepared. But then I feel a hand on mine, and I meet Sook's gaze. It's warm and familiar and seems to say: *You've got this.*

I breathe out. "Um, I'm really good friends with Sook and Malka, and they needed a violinist, so it was a perfect fit. And I'm really, um, passionate about music."

"Who are some of your influences?" Rasha asks.

I shift in my seat. "I grew up listening to classic rock and jam bands, and I guess that's still my favorite sound." I pause, thinking of all the music I appreciate. "But some of the orchestral pieces I play are great also. I guess a lot of instrumental stuff, which works well because Sook is a great composer." She beams at me as I continue. "It's like she has five instruments going in her head at once. It's kind of awesome."

The rest of the segment flies by. Rasha wraps, and then we're all standing and shaking hands with each other. Rasha waves in Amir.

"Great job," he says.

Sook twists her hands together. "So it sounded okay?"

"It sounded fantastic!"

"Hey, little brother," Rasha says, which is funny since he has almost six inches on her.

They hug, and then Amir steps back to stand beside her. "It'll be a great episode. Some of the people on here are so boring, it's painful."

"Wow," Rasha says sarcastically. "Thanks for the vote of confidence in the show."

"It's a vote of confidence in you," he responds. "I know you didn't produce any of those segments."

"You know what would be an interesting episode? Talking about your photography!"

Amir's smile falters, but he shifts and says, "Speaking of photography, I'm heading to a showing near campus, at Elaine's, if anyone would like to join me."

"Hmm, what do y'all think?" Sook asks.

"Well," Rasha says, "I don't drink, but these places tend to have free wine and no hesitation to serve minors."

"Free wine? Oh, we're definitely in," Malka says.

"You interested, Ariel?" Amir asks. He reaches up to scratch his neck, and his shirt rises, revealing a bit of his stomach. Brown skin and a dusting of fine hairs.

I swallow hard. "Sure. I'm in."

"It's weird to drink wine without praying first," I murmur to Malka. We're standing in front of a giant photograph on canvas. It's a simple picture, a field with a glimpse of a small hand and a girl's dress on the side, just out of the camera's focus. It gives me this strange urge to run after her and see what she's chasing out of frame.

Malka laughs. "Yeah, getting drunk the first time on something other than Manischewitz was also weird, but don't worry"—she pats my arm—"you'll adjust."

We're a couple miles from campus at Elaine's. I understand why Amir loves this place. The rooms are minimal but warm, the crowd is quiet but friendly, and acoustic guitar plays from hidden speakers. The song playing now sounds like a stripped-down version of "Blackbird" by the Beatles.

All five of us carpooled here from the studio. If you'd asked me a month ago who I'd be hanging out with on a Friday night and what I'd be doing with them, this would not have been my answer. I wonder if this is what college is like, going with the flow, always saying yes because who really cares about that waiting pile of homework. It's remarkable, the possibility in even one free Friday.

Amir is working his way around the room, shaking hands and talking with people. He's comfortable here, assured. People seem to gravitate toward him.

I try not to focus on each guy who shakes his hand or claps him on the back. I wonder if Jacob the twenty-two-year-old photographer is around.

"You're staring again," Malka whispers.

"Hmm?" I go to take a sip of my wine, but the little cup is empty. "Want some more? I need to, um, cleanse my palate before the next photo."

"I don't think that's a thing," Malka says.

"It's definitely not."

We grab more wine anyway and then move onto the next photo. And the next after that. After a bit, Malka says to take my time. There's a little pocket park next to the gallery, and she's going to hang there with Rasha and Sook.

I trail around the room on my own, enjoying wine that

doesn't taste like grape juice and art that isn't asking anything of me. There's a spotlight section, a single wall for a new artist. Her work complements the rest of the gallery well. I settle in front of a photo of a night sky. A silhouette blurs at the bottom of the frame, perhaps someone dancing under the stars. "This is one of my favorites," a familiar voice says.

Spearmint and basil.

I glance at Amir. He's standing close to me, staring at the photo. "It's nice," I say. "It makes me feel content."

"At ease. Too many photos are dark, depressing. As if only serious subjects make good art. I think it's harder to make someone happy than make them sad."

"Yeah." I nod. "I guess that's true."

"C'mon." His hand brushes against my arm. "I want to show you a few more."

I'm glad the girls are gone. Everything about this moment feels too indulgent to share. We wander around the gallery together. My skin tingles. I want to take his hand.

He's wearing a cardigan over a T-shirt. He pulls the combo off well—he looks hot. But I narrow my eyes at his Hufflepuff shirt.

"I thought you were a Ravenclaw," I say.

"Observant." He grins. "I'm a Ravenpuff, so I wear both."

I shake my head. "I love Harry Potter, but I haven't put that much thought into my house."

"Hmm, I'd say you're a Gryffinclaw."

"I'll get my two shirts." I sip the last of my wine. "How often do you come to these shows?"

We're now standing in a dark corner of the exhibit. A single light shines on a photo of a moth hovering above a lantern. Our shoulders are close, touching in the most imperceptible way. I swear he leans toward me. I swallow, not wanting to move and break the moment. "Not as much as I'd like," he says. "But at least a couple of times a month."

"Do you go alone or with a friend or a…boyfriend?" I almost cough out the last word.

"No boyfriend. I usually go alone and run into friends." He glances at me, smiling. "But I'm enjoying the company tonight."

———————————

The scent of the food arrives before the plates. My mouth waters. The Thai restaurant is small and dark. We're all squeezed into a booth in the back. A few tea lights illuminate the lacquered black table. I'm in the far corner with Amir next to me. Rasha and Malka are across from us, and Sook sits at the head of the table. Rasha told us she comes here at least once a week.

Our waitress sets the dishes on the table. Piles of noodles with spiced beef and sliced peppers. Rice with egg and scallions and shredded tofu. I put my face over my plate and inhale the scented steam. It is *literally* mouthwatering. The perfect second dinner.

Amir picks up his fork. He ordered the ginger chicken in a light brown sauce with skinny sautéed onions. "Ariel," he says. "Stop checking out my food."

I laugh. "I can't help it." But I pick up my fork and turn to my own plate.

Rasha grins at me from across the table. "Get ready for the rest of the food in your life to disappoint you forever."

I take a bite. Damn, that's good. I've never had Thai like this. Spicy and sweet with a hint of acid from the lime. The noodles are cooked perfectly, and the beef is soft and seasoned.

"Hello, please bury me in this restaurant because I'm never leaving," I say.

"I'll be buried in the plot next to you," Amir agrees.

Our table lapses into satiated silence as everyone dives into their dishes. It reminds me of that five-minute window when we have guests over for Shabbat dinner. We're a family of talkers, but when Mom's matzo ball soup descends upon us, no one has time for conversation.

We all finish, one after another. I lean back in the booth, staring at my demolished plate. Amir reclines next to me, our shoulders pushed together. The booth is small. They have to be touching. Okay, I might be leaning into him a little bit.

"I really wanted leftovers." His plate is as empty as mine. "I might be driving back tomorrow for more."

"Smart. Take me with you," I say.

"Okay." He smiles, and my skin flushes. I know he's joking, but still...Amir and I going out to a restaurant alone? A cozy, dim, intimate restaurant?

Something brushes my hand. I look down. Amir's fingers sweep over mine. I glance at everyone around us, but no one can see under the low table. Our fingers intertwine, grip, lock. I stare at the table, trying to keep a neutral face, as his hand squeezes mine.

God, I want to kiss him.

We slip back into the group conversation. But all the laughter and chatter feel distant, filtered. All I can concentrate on is the heat of our clasped hands.

Eventually, it gets late. The restaurant empties out. Our waitress gives us the *I want to finish my shift* sigh. "I'll go get the car," Amir offers since it's parked about eight blocks away.

Without a second thought, I say, "I'll go with you."

Only Malka gives us a suspicious look. Sook and Rasha say thanks and go back to their conversation.

A minute later, I'm alone with Amir. We walk down the lamp-lit sidewalks. I miss his hand already, but it feels too real to hold it out here. Amir has gone quiet again. A contemplative quiet, but I'm bursting with adrenaline, with the need to make something happen. I keep glancing at his lips.

"I had fun tonight," I finally say. "Much better than studying at home."

"Good, I'm glad." Amir looks at me. His eyes are warmer than ever in the lamplight. I search them for a moment, wondering if he feels what I do.

Curiosity fuels courage. "Maybe we could do it again. By ourselves. If you know of other shows..."

"I'd like that."

We slip back into silence, but the air crackles between us. When we get to the car, Amir follows me around to the passenger side. He stands in front of me, hands tucked into his pockets. My back almost touches the car. I try to take a calming breath but inhale spearmint and basil.

"Ariel?" Amir asks. His gaze is sincere and resolute. "Can I kiss you?"

My throat catches, voice coming out rough. "Yeah, you can kiss me."

Our lips meet, and it's soft and sweet with a flicker of need. Amir tugs my jacket, bringing me closer to him. Our chests press together lightly, and my pulse jumps.

It's the gentlest kiss in the world. Determined in its leisure, like we can stay here against his car for an eternity. His lips brush against mine and then wander to my cheek and jaw, featherlight. My hands instinctively reach for his hair. It's full and soft, and Amir makes a little noise when I run my fingers through it.

Eventually, his mouth returns to my lips, one final kiss.

Then he leans his forehead against mine, and I open my eyes just to see him that near. His eyes are still closed, eyelashes long and dark.

Amir pulls back but only a bit. He nudges me, wearing an unbearably earnest smile, and says, "You know, Ariel, I'm really glad you're bad at calculus."

"Oh my god." I laugh, then shove him gently, but my hand bunches against his shirt, holding him to me. "That's terrible."

"Is it?"

"Yes," I say. Then I tug him forward and kiss him again.

NINE

"Rachel, can you grab some extra soap from the storage closet?" I call out. I'm elbow-deep in the sink, washing a sweet little mutt.

No response.

"Rachel?" I call louder.

"Ugh. One minute."

She stalks into the room a few moments later and drops the soap on the counter. "Here, happy?" She turns on her heel and leaves.

"You are way too young to be turning into a teenager!" I yell after her.

An hour later, I'm finished washing all the dogs, but I'm not at all tired. My lips are still buzzing from kissing Amir last night. I could've stayed like that, back pressed against the car, all evening. But our friends probably would've noticed if we never picked them up.

It's only been fourteen hours since I saw him, but it already feels like too long. I'll be at services instead of school Monday and Tuesday, so what if I don't get to see him until Wednesday? When will I get to kiss him again? *Will* I get to kiss him again?

I'm assuming it wasn't a one-off.

It definitely didn't *feel* like a one-off.

I went straight to bed when I got home last night, a crash after all the adrenaline, and slept for eight hours before waking up for shul. Maybe I can see Amir tomorrow. Rachel doesn't have a soccer game because of the upcoming high holidays, so tomorrow my only commitment is practice with Dizzy Daisies.

I grab Ezekiel from his cage and head to the front room. "Want to go play with him outside?" I ask Rachel.

She's on the couch, reading from a folder, brow furrowed. Her backpack is stuffed in her lap, and she's hugging it like a pillow.

"What are you working on?" I ask. "Pirates? Capitals?"

"Reading sheets." Rachel flips a page. She nibbles one of her sweatshirt drawstrings.

"Want to take a break? Play with the dogs?"

"I'm gonna keep working," she says, not looking up at me.

"C'mon, it'll be fun."

"I'm working, Ariel. I don't want to get behind."

I guess even fifth graders have catch-up work for missing two days of class. Still, I hesitate. But then Ezekiel yaps at my heels, little tail wagging.

"Okay," I say. "We'll be out there if you want to join us."

I grab my phone and take Ezekiel out into the yard.

"That's a lot of sheet music," I say when Sook hands me a stack of papers. It's Sunday afternoon, and we're in her basement for our first practice together. This morning Amir texted, and we made plans to study tonight at my place. I keep glancing at my phone, watching the minutes tick by until evening.

"Well, obviously," Sook says. "This isn't one of your jam bands. I wasn't going to let you make up the notes."

I leaf through the pages. "But this is *a lot* of sheet music."

"I figured I'd add you into a few of the songs. You know, just in case. If you like playing with us."

It looks like she's written me parts for at least half their repertoire. "*Sook,*" I warn.

Malka scrambles down the stairs. She's holding a bagel in her mouth while she throws her hair up into a messy bun.

"Oh, good," Sook says. "I was about to text you."

"Sorry I'm late," Malka responds. "My roommate dragged me to my first frat party last night, so you know, hangover. Getting out of bed today was basically the worst thing to ever happen to me."

"Are you good now? Maybe go chug some water?" Sook taps her fingers against her keyboard.

"How was the party?" I ask. "Did you have fun?"

Malka scrunches up her face. "It was kind of disgusting. The house was gross, all sticky and dark. And they made some kind of punch in a giant trash can, I'm not even kidding you. All the guys were loud and wasted. *So* not cute. Not my scene."

"Gross," I say. "So none of it was fun?"

"Well, my friends and I found a corner and an unopened bottle of flavored vodka, so we drank that. And after we were *quite* drunk, we all went to Waffle House together, and *that* was fun. Awesome waffles. Life-changing waffles."

"So in college, we should only ever get drunk so we get to drunk-eat?"

Malka laughs. "Yeah, basically."

"So…get that water?" Sook cuts in. "So we can start practice?"

Malka gives her a look, then tightly says, "Yep. Be right back."

"Thank you!" Sook replies. As Malka ascends the stairs, Sook shoves her face in her hands and groans.

"What's wrong?" I ask.

She drags her hands down so I can see her eyes. "I know I'm being annoying. I can *hear* myself being annoying." She pauses. "This deal my parents gave me…I know I sound ridiculous, complaining about having to go to an Ivy League school. It's spoiled and privileged and absurd." She bites her lip. "But this is my dream and my chance to pursue it. I don't *want* to be the person nagging everyone all the time, but if we don't practice, we won't get better, and then we won't find an agent, and my music career will be over before it even starts." Her voice cracks on the last word, and she tears up. "It's ridiculous. *I'm ridiculous.*"

"Hey," I say, walking over to her. I sit on the stool next to hers and pat her back.

Sook gives me a wry grin. "What am I? One of the dogs at your shelter?"

"Want me to scratch behind your ear?"

She laughs and shoves me off. "Oh my god, no."

I laugh back and knock into her shoulder. "Don't be so hard on yourself. You aren't ridiculous. You know what you want. But maybe"—I pause—"maybe you're being a bit harsh with Malka. Let her know what's going on with you. See if she wants the same things."

Sook wrings her hands together. "But what if she doesn't?"

"That will suck. But it's better than ruining your friendship."

She puts her head down and groans one more time. I pat her back again.

"I need this to happen," she mumbles. She tilts her head, and her eyes meet mine. "If I don't pursue my dream now, I'll lose it. I'll go off to Dartmouth, and I'll study and get a real job and pay bills and get married, and I'll never prioritize my music again. I know I'm only in high school, but it's like I'm already running out of time."

Her words echo my own spiral of thoughts. If I don't get

into Harvard, my whole life will be running to catch an opportunity I already missed.

I'm tempted to let Sook in. Confide in her like I confided in Amir. But my problems are over, right? I aced the last test. I don't need to complain about an issue that no longer exists.

Malka's footsteps pad down the stairs, and I nudge Sook and whisper, "Talk to her."

"Almost ready, promise," Malka says, sipping her water and seeming tense.

Sook glances up. "It's okay, take your time."

Malka narrows her eyes. "Why?"

"Look." Sook clears her throat. "I'm sorry I've been uptight about the band and not the nicest person to be around." She glances at Malka. "I really want this, you know. And I only have like half a year to make it happen. But I know you're in college and have this other life now, and I need to be considerate of that."

Malka looks stunned, but her face softens. "Thank you, for apologizing. Really. I"—she pauses—"I love this band, but do I want it to be my first priority? Do I want to get signed and pursue this for real?"

"Do you?" Sook asks.

Malka hesitates. "Truthfully, I don't know. I don't want to commit and say yes and then screw you over."

Sook twists her mouth. "Yeah, I don't want you to screw me over, either."

"Can I promise to stay honest with you? If I'm ever starting to doubt my commitment, I'll let you know and give you time to find someone new?"

"That's really fair, and I really hate that. I love you, Malka."

"I love you, too," she responds.

"This is like the happy ending of a Disney Channel Original Movie," I say, grinning.

"Shut up," both of them respond.

"Okay, but if I shut up, I can't tell you my news." My pulse skips just from teasing them. I can still feel the gentle press of Amir's lips against mine.

Malka grins. "I think I know what this news will be."

"What?" Sook looks confused. "Am I missing something? I'm missing something." She stands. "What am I missing, Ariel? Tell me!"

"Amir and I kissed. Friday night. When we went to get the car."

Malka squeals. "I knew it! Like you wanted to walk to the car with him out of nowhere. Yeah, right. Y'all could barely keep your eyes off each other at dinner."

"Oy," I groan. "Were we really that obvious?"

"Obviously not that obvious," Sook says. "I had no clue." She narrows her eyes. "I thought you didn't like him. What's going on?"

"I didn't not—I mean, yeah, he annoyed me. But I don't

know. We started hanging out because…" I hesitate. "We wanted to study for calculus. And we got along better than expected, and one thing led to another, and…" My smile is too big. I pick up a pillow and hide my face with it.

"Oh my god, adorable," Malka says. "Y'all make a cute couple."

"A couple?" Sook asks. "You guys are dating?"

"No!" I say. "I mean, no, not yet. We only kissed a couple days ago, and we haven't talked about it, but we're going to study again tonight so…"

"Okay," Sook says. "Cool."

I stare at her. "Your enthusiasm is lacking."

"Sorry."

I stare more.

She holds her hands up and smiles, eyes wide. "Sorry! I mean it! I'm happy for you guys. I just need time to adjust. I had no clue. Admittedly, I feel kind of left out, Ariel. You didn't tell me you were into him. I told you about my crush on Clarissa, and she doesn't even live in this city."

She's right.

"You're right." I scratch my ear. "It happened really fast. I didn't tell anyone. Forgive me, best friend?"

"But of course." She wraps an arm around my shoulder. "I'm happy for you, really. Now come on. It's time to actually play our instruments."

We set up. It feels weird to have my violin in a new

environment. I crack all my knuckles, then my neck. I practiced my Rimsky-Korsakov solo for hours yesterday, so my fingers are sore from the metal strings. It's going to be a rough week keeping up practice for the solo and the band.

I read over the sheet music. It's much easier than what we're playing in orchestra, but there's this different kind of pressure. Sook and Malka are practically professionals now. What if I'm not good enough? What if at the end of this session, Sook turns and says, "Thanks very much, but never mind. I'm going to give Pari a call"?

But I don't have time for nerves because Sook is counting us off, and then she leads in with Malka. It's the new song, the one I loved last session, the one where I could hear the opening for a violin. When my time approaches, I set my violin, tuck my chin, and bring the bow to the string.

The first note wavers, hesitant. But then I pull the next ones out, one by one. The violin is both sweet and growling like the rest of the song.

The music drifts around the room, atmospheric and entrancing. We get through the song, and I play vibrato on the final, ringing note. My body hums. I can't remember the last time I fell into a piece of music like this.

"Not bad," Malka says, smiling.

"Could be better." Sook grins.

"Can we play it again?" I ask.

Sook winks. "On the count."

Later that night, I'm home alone and practicing in my room. The rest of the family is at a friend's house for dinner, but I begged off earlier today, mentioning practice might run late. And it did run late. After a few run-throughs, my classic rock background had an itch, and I suggested a couple of harder riffs for the transitions. Sook approved the idea, and it worked great. I felt that burst of satisfaction, like when I get a perfect score.

But blisters have formed, both on my fingers from the press of the metal strings and my neck from holding the violin in place. I've got to push through and take advantage of my long weekend to practice this orchestra solo. Acing that calculus test has relieved a lot of pressure, but my college applications still feel bare without soccer. Maybe I should've signed up for debate or ran for student government. I've got to keep orchestra to look well-rounded, and I've got to keep first chair to stand out from all the other well-rounded students.

I adjust the sheet music. Then I take a small brick of rosin and slide it across my bow's horsehair. It's ritual, all the little steps that go into playing. The tuning, the rosin, the tock of the metronome.

Once done, I lift my violin and focus on the page. I can do this. I take a breath and imagine the prelude. Cellos plucking. Violas singing. All leading up to my solo, and then I hear the oboe play its final notes, and I begin, blistered fingers against metal strings, playing painful, perfect notes.

The solo picks up, fast yet airy, and I can hear the accompaniment join me. We build and play through the piece together.

And then, when it's over, I relax my stance and breathe.

It wasn't good enough.

Dr. Whitmore's voice echoes in my head: "Again."

I play the *Scheherazade* solo over and over. Each time I hit the notes a bit more precisely, each time my bow swipes across the strings with more control, each time my fingers burn with more pain, but it's a distant feeling. Unimportant. This is how it's supposed to be. This is how first chair practices. Gives it everything, body and soul. I'm about to bear down on the solo once more when there's a knock on my bedroom door.

I startle.

Are my parents home already?

"Mom?" I call cautiously.

"No, it's me."

Amir? I rub my eyes. How did I forget he was coming over?

"Ariel?"

"Coming!" I open the door, and there he is, Amir, outside my bedroom. He's wearing black sweatpants. They sling low on his hips. I swallow hard.

"Sorry, the garage was open, and you weren't picking up

your phone. I heard you playing from downstairs. You sound good." He holds up his textbook. "Still want to study?"

I'm home alone with Amir. Amir who is wearing those sweatpants. "Um, yeah. Let's study. Come in." I let him into my room. The silence makes my thudding pulse too loud, so I tap my phone and play *Scheherazade*. The strings fill the room.

I scratch my ear. "So, do you—"

"You're bleeding," Amir says.

"What?"

He steps closer to me, gaze on my neck. And then his fingers are there, tracing the delicate skin. I shiver. His fingers travel down my arm, then to my fingers. Also bleeding. Only a few drops. I've seen worse. He lifts his hand, as if to show proof.

"Oh," I say.

"Yeah," he says.

He's standing close to me, eyes not breaking contact.

And then the music lifts and we're kissing. I'm not sure who leans in first. Maybe both of us, but his lips are on mine, and I'm inhaling him, spearmint and basil.

It's hungrier than our first kiss.

My arms wrap around his back, feeling his broad shoulders. And I draw him close to me. His lips leave mine and run down my jaw and neck before finding my mouth once more. We step back together, then back again, until his legs press against the edge of my bed. *Scheherazade* delves deeper into the first movement. My pulse races to catch up with the tempo.

I pull back for a second, breathing hard.

"You okay?" Amir asks.

My hands tangle with his, like I'm unable to break complete contact. "I'm okay, but uh—" I clear my throat, glancing back at my bed. "I don't want to have sex or anything. I mean, I do, like one day, but I don't want to have sex right now."

"Me neither," Amir says. I exhale. He scratches his neck, self-conscious for a rare moment. "Pants stay on?"

"Pants stay on," I agree.

We both smile.

Then we're kissing again. Then we're on the bed kissing, twisting and pushing closer together. I pull my lips across his skin, against the stubble of his jaw, down his neck, and across his collarbone. Amir shudders beneath me as I accidentally nip the skin.

Too hot. He is actually too hot of a person.

"This okay?" he asks, reaching for the hem of my T-shirt.

"Yeah." I'm a bit breathless as he pulls my shirt off and then his also. I'm overwhelmed by the press of his bare chest against mine.

We slow down, more like our first kiss. Lingering in the moment, kisses as wandering as our conversations. Time slips by, and we only pull apart when *Scheherazade* ends and the room drops into silence.

I lean my head against his bare chest and breathe him in. My hand runs down his skin. There's a spot of my dried blood from earlier. I rub it away, then kiss the spot. He makes a soft hum in response.

I blink, my eyes half-closed, suddenly sated and sleepy. "I don't want to go to services tomorrow," I say. "I want to stay right here."

"I wish I had a Time-Turner like Hermione. Think about it. We could keep turning back the clock and stay here as long as we want."

"I could be into that."

"Will your parents be home soon?"

"We have some time." I look down at our bare chests. "But maybe we should put our shirts back on." I pause. "Should we tell them?"

Amir shifts so he can glance at me. "Tell them what?"

He's grinning, teasing me. He wants me to say it. "I don't know," I say. "That we're hanging. Talking."

He traces a finger across my collarbone. "I think we're doing a bit more than talking."

I blush. "Maybe we should wait."

"Maybe," he agrees. "I'll be here tomorrow, by the way. Your mom invited us for Rosh Hashanah dinner."

"Let's *definitely* wait then," I say. "We'll be animals in a zoo if we tell them before we all spend the evening together."

"Good call," Amir agrees. The air-conditioning clicks on, the cold air blasting the room. Amir pulls the blanket up so it covers us. It's warm under here, snug. "We'll keep the invisibility cloak on for now," Amir says.

I snort. *"Nerd."*

Amir grins. *"Dork."*

TEN

The benches creak as everyone rises to their feet for the Amidah. "Baruch atah Adonai, eloheinu veilohei avoteinu, elohei Avraham, elohei Yitzchak, veilohei Yaakov…"

The prayer continues. I have it memorized from years of repetition, so I recite it as I look around the room. The synagogue is packed for Rosh Hashanah, the Jewish New Year. Many of our congregants only attend shul for the High Holidays. Our sanctuary even has removable dividers so we can expand the space to twice the size.

Voices boom around me, the entire congregation joining together in something more powerful than song. It's always comforting, being surrounded by so many people reciting the same prayers as the generations before us.

As the Amidah switches to the silent portion, I think of Amir, up in my bedroom last night. The back of my neck heats.

I slip out my phone, keeping it low and against my thigh. No messages. I refresh my email. Even though it's usually spam, every time a new email from a college pops up, my heart jolts, and I panic and wonder if I'm forgetting something.

People are beginning to sit, so I do also. My parents are still praying. Mom mouths the Hebrew, and Dad traces the English translation with his finger. I glance at Rachel. She's playing with a rubber band, twisting and stretching it, hands never stilling.

My phone buzzes. A calendar reminder to prepare for my Harvard interview, which is in less than two weeks. I scan the calendar: calculus quiz, gov test, paper for Spanish lit, college essay, practice violin solo, work on college applications...

Maybe I have more work to do this weekend than I'd thought.

The prayer finishes and another begins.

———————

Everyone mills around after services. Rachel runs off to play at Tinder Hill, and Mom and Dad say Happy New Year to a hundred different people. They're connected to every family through some good deed, from reporting on a health crisis at a school to representing families pro bono. They do so much for the community and ask for nothing in return. My volunteer hours at the shelter are a pittance in comparison.

I find Malka in the tide of congregants, and we wander up and down the mostly deserted preschool branch of the synagogue. We peer into one of the classrooms, with its map of Israel and toys and miniature tables and chairs.

Malka laughs and squats down into one of the tiny seats. "Can you believe we were ever this little?"

"Nope," I say, sitting also, my butt not even half fitting.

"I remember you both being that little," a new voice chimes in. Rabbi Solomon stands in the doorway, holding her lavender tallis bag.

"Rabbi!" Malka says. "L'shana Tova!"

"L'shana Tova, Malka. L'shana Tova, Ariel."

"Shana Tova!" I respond. "I enjoyed your sermon."

Rabbi Solomon raises an eyebrow. "I wasn't sure if you caught it with your phone out."

Malka snickers and says, "Ooooh," like we really are kids again.

My cheeks flame red. "Sorry, I was listening. I promise."

Rabbi Solomon waves her hand dismissively. "That's all right. Come with me, you two. Ariel, I have something to give you."

"Are you sure?" I ask, though I'm curious what she has for me. "Aren't you busy today?"

"*Too busy*. I need to hide, and you two will be my buffer until we get to my office. Act like we're in a very intense conversation, fershtay?"

Malka and I nod, both amused. Our rabbi has us pulling a con. We walk down the hallway on either side of her. Sure enough, everyone we pass tries to get her attention.

"Wonderful sermon, Rabbi Solomon, I wanted to ask—"

"Rabbi Solomon, how are your—"

"Oh good, Rabbi, solve this debate for us—"

We take turns cutting people off. Rabbi Solomon is the most adept at it, though. She raises one finger, looks serious, and says, "I'm so sorry. I'm in the middle of something important with these young ones." And then we keep moving down the hall. I've never gotten through a crowd at synagogue so fast.

We make it to her office, and she breathes an overdramatic sigh of relief as she shuts the door behind us. "Baruch Hashem," she says. "We made it."

Her office is large. There's enough space for a six-person table, plus her desk and two giant armchairs. Bookcases take up most of the wall space, filled with texts, both in Hebrew and English. Judaica also lines the shelves, from ornate, expensive pieces to bits of sculpted clay from the preschoolers. Rabbi Solomon tutored me here for my bar mitzvah, a few one-on-one sessions to critique my D'var Torah.

I remember enjoying it. Her questions and critiques pushed me to learn and grow. And it was nice improving my speech simply to improve it, not for a grade.

"Here we are." Rabbi Solomon plucks a book from the

shelf. "It's a shortened version of the Talmud. The one I had growing up as a girl was too bulky, so it never left our coffee table. But this could easily fit in a book bag or even a purse. I brought my copy to university and read it there. Before I knew it, I was reading from the Talmud every day. Of course, then I ran out of stories and moved on to the big book. I like to give every graduating student an abridged copy."

"Thank you," I say, taking the book, feeling a bit guilty it will likely go home to sit on my shelf. But Rabbi Solomon did say it's for college, so maybe I'll have time to read it next year.

"Malka, are you enjoying yours? How's college?"

"I am." She tucks her hair behind her ears. She's wearing gold hoops today, and her lips are coated in some kind of gloss. "I read a few stories. They were good. And college is…great!" She clears her throat, looking like she wants to change the subject. "I went to the campus Chabad. They were nice."

Rabbi Solomon clasps her hands together. "That's wonderful to hear! I love Rabbi Shmul! He's done a fantastic job getting the students involved."

"Yeah," Malka says. "I like him."

"Wonderful, wonderful. I like hearing our young ones are investing in their community. Those relationships will last you a lifetime." She glances at the time on her watch and tsks. "I should probably get back to the masses. Thank you both for providing me a respite." She smiles. "And again, L'Shana Tova."

"Don't do it!" Sook squeals.

Rachel cackles and chases Sook across the kitchen, fingers coated with honey. "I'm coming for you!"

"Make it stop!" Sook hollers.

"On it!" I intercept and pick Rachel up by her armpits, bringing her to my eye level. She grins wickedly. "Don't," I warn. But she plants her sticky palm flat against my cheek. "Ugh, now you're going to get it."

I put her down and snatch the dish of apples and honey from the table. Holding it high above her reach, I swipe honey onto my finger and dash after her around the dining room table, but before I can get to her, the front door opens, and I stop short in front of Rasha and Amir.

Amir looks exceptionally amused. "Happy New Year," he says.

"Thanks," I respond, breathless. Our eyes lock for a long moment, and I swallow hard.

Rasha looks back and forth between us. "Something is going on here. Are y'all like…"

"Shh!" We both shush her at the same time.

"We haven't had a chance to tell the parents," Amir says.

"We will. Soon."

"It's new," Amir continues. "We don't need them planning a wedding before Ariel takes me out on a date."

"Oh, I'm taking *you* out on a date?"

"Well, the photography show was my idea, so it's your turn. Better be good, too."

"Challenge accepted."

"Whoa," Rasha says. "So this really is happening." She glances back and forth between us, then nods. "Okay, cool. I ship it."

I grin. "Good. I'm gonna go shower off. There's honey everywhere."

"Everywhere?" Amir asks.

"Oh my god," Rasha groans, while I blush.

Upstairs, I shower fast, body humming with endorphins and nerves. I still have a lot of work left, but all I really want to do is spend more time with Amir. I step out of my bathroom, towel wrapped around my waist, then freeze. Malka, Sook, Rasha, and Amir are all hanging out in my room.

"Hi, guys," I say. "Please. Come in."

They all laugh. "Sorry, dude," Malka says. "It was getting a little grown-up heavy down there."

"Yeah, really couldn't deal with one more person asking me where I'm applying to school," Sook says.

"Or how I like college," Rasha says.

"Or how my dorm is," Malka says.

"Or where I'm applying to school," Amir finishes, but his voice is higher than usual, and he's very intently *not* looking at me in my towel.

"Understandable. I'm gonna, uh—" I slide open my dresser drawers and grab some clothes. "Change. I'll be right back."

Ten minutes later, we're playing Settlers of Catan on my bedroom floor. I love this game and haven't had time to play since summer. Amir has never played because he, unsurprisingly, prefers Harry Potter Clue, but he picks it up with ease. It becomes apparent Rasha is a mastermind of Catan.

We pick at my stash of candy as we play, Haribo Sour S'ghetti and Peaches. The game passes by quickly with laughter and shouts of "Longest road!" and "Don't knight me!"

Amir is stretched out on his stomach next to me, head propped on his arm, laughing as Rasha and Sook barter with wheat and sheep. He glances my way, and I fizz with pleasure.

Before I know it, we're being called downstairs for dinner. I glance out the window into the fading light. I'll have to get some work done after everyone leaves, maybe stay up a bit late, but that's okay. I don't need much sleep to sit through morning services. Most kids don't even go to synagogue on the second day of Rosh Hashanah. Some because they're not as observant and some because it's so difficult to miss one day of school, much less two. But in my family, both days are mandatory.

We all file downstairs. The house booms with loud voices and laughter. There are a couple dozen people here for dinner. Malka and Sook's parents. Amir's entire family. A few other couples from shul. My parents' cousins. Everyone greets me, a blur of hugs and handshakes and kisses on the cheek.

"L'Shanna Tova!"

"Happy New Year!"

"Shana Tova!"

It's warm in the kitchen, and the smell of matzo ball soup and brisket wafts toward me. Amir joins his family at the counter, as my parents ladle out bowls of soup.

Mr. Naeem wraps an arm around Amir. "Be sure to remember the name Amir Naeem," he says to Mrs. Rifkin from shul. "He's going to be a famous photographer."

"In all the galleries, I know it," Mrs. Naeem agrees. "He's a genius with the lens."

Amir forces a half smile, and my heart tugs. He must feel me staring because he glances up. I nod toward the dining room, and he excuses himself and heads that way, passing me with a quick grin.

I grab two bowls of soup from Mom and Dad. They're pulling the same crap. *Ariel is applying to Harvard*, Mom says. My jaw tenses. Sometimes it feels like it's the only thing they say about me, like it's the only interesting thing about me, the only thing worth being proud of. At Passover Seder, will they be telling the same people, *No, he didn't get in?*

I join Amir in the dining room. It's still mostly empty in here, and the few people sitting are busy devouring their soup.

Amir and I grab seats at the end of the table. His eyes light up. "Is this what I think it is?"

"Jewish penicillin, the best food in existence. Yes, it is my mother's matzo ball soup."

"That's quite the intro."

"I haven't even begun to do this soup justice." The scent of dill and salty kosher chicken drifts between us. "God, I'm jealous of you. I wish I could remember my first time, but Mom probably fed me the broth in a bottle as a baby."

"Is it better than the Thai food?"

"It is better than *all* food. It is another plane of existence. Like there's food, and there's great food, and then in another galaxy far, far away there's matzo ball soup."

I angle my chair so I can watch Amir. I'm suddenly anxious. What if he doesn't like it? Obviously, we can't date if he doesn't like matzo ball soup.

Amir looks at me. "I feel like whatever reaction I have isn't going to be big enough."

"Okay, I'm chilling. Promise." I cross my arms and lean back in my chair. "See? I'm chill."

"Mm-hmm, sure." Amir eyes me with suspicion. "All right, here we go."

He lifts his spoon and sips. His eyes widen. He stares down at the bowl, then takes another sip. Then he glances up at me for only a second before taking another spoonful and another.

"Take a bite of the matzo—"

I start to say, but Amir is already spooning off part of the matzo ball and trying it, a bit of carrot and shredded chicken, too. Before I know it, his entire bowl is finished. He looks up at me, eyes full of wonder. Finally, he gives a Jewish mother's favorite praise: "Please tell me I can have seconds."

Later that night, after all the guests have left, my family is collapsed in the living room. Dad snores in the armchair, too tired to make it upstairs. One of his slippers has fallen off.

"Oy gevalt, remind me to never host the High Holidays again," Mom says, yawning. Her feet are propped up on a pillow on Rachel's lap, and Rachel is massaging them for her.

"You say that every year," I respond, while reading AP Gov notes off my phone. So far, thanks to the detailed presentations our teacher posts online, I haven't had to open a textbook for the class, and I am *so* not complaining. "And then every year you say you'll have a low-key dinner, and you won't make a big fuss, and then you end up inviting the entire tribe, and we end up here, with your ten-year-old daughter rubbing your feet."

"I don't mind!" Rachel says. "I will always rub feet for matzo ball soup."

I tap away from my notes and pull up my calendar. The Harvard application is looming closer, but at least I'm back on the right track. I'll use my last day off school to practice for my violin solo, and I can also get ahead in my reading for Spanish lit.

"Thank you, mamaleh," Mom says. "Ariel, did your friends enjoy the soup?"

"They always do," I answer.

"What about Amir? Did he like the soup?"

I freeze. She knows. How does she know? "Um…"

"Amir's mom mentioned he hadn't tried it before. He had some tonight, right? Do you know if he liked it?"

"Oh," I say, clearing my throat. "Yeah, he did. I mean, I think so. It's your soup. Everyone likes it."

"That's good. And how long have you two been dating?"

Oh shit.

That was good.

"Um."

"*You're dating Amir?*" Rachel squeals.

"Well, we…how did you…."

"Mrs. Naeem and I always said you two would be cute together. Now when did this start? I noticed you talking at Rachel's game. You know we support that you're gay, right?"

I clear my throat. "Bisexual."

"Yes, right! I'm sorry. That's what I meant—I don't care that you're bisexual. I mean, I do care. In a good way."

I give her a soft smile. "I know."

My parents were pretty great when I came out in ninth

grade. There was a lot of hugging and thankfully not a lot of questions. Mom took a while to understand the guys *and* girls part, which to be fair, took me a while to get myself. I know she's trying, though, and I know Amir and I are ridiculously lucky to have parents who *want* their sons to date.

"So." Mom nudges me. "How long have you two been going out?"

My face flushes, but I guess it's better to rip off the Band-Aid. I should've known she'd figure it out sooner rather than later. "We're not *going out*, but yeah, we're talking or whatever... it's new." I rub my face. I'm so not prepared to define the relationship, much less with my mom instead of Amir. "Can we maybe leave it alone for now?"

Mom smiles. "Yes, yes we can. For now." She sighs and settles back into the couch. "Rachel, could I bother you to grab the lotion from my bathroom?"

"That depends." Rachel has a scheming look in her eye. "Can I bring leftover soup for lunch Wednesday? My teacher will let me use the microwave!"

"Deal," Mom says.

My phone buzzes as they shake hands. It's a text from Amir. *Warning: the parents know*

I laugh. *Yep. That didn't take long. We're great at secrets*

He responds: *Basically, we should be secret agents*

It only makes sense

"That Amir?" Mom asks in time for me to realize I have the most ridiculous smile on my face.

"*Mom,*" I groan.

She laughs and extends her foot to nudge my leg. "Love you, tatala."

"Love you, too," I mutter, cheeks red, still smiling.

ELEVEN

Wednesday morning rushes by in a blur of catch-up assignments. I always ask my teachers to provide the work ahead of time, but few prepare to help the handful of Jewish students in their classes. By the time I get to English, I know it's going to require a late night to get all of it done. And my family is going to Amir's house for dinner, so I won't even get started until after eight. At least I'll see Amir. Maybe we'll have time to sneak off for a few minutes.

Sook is bubbling over as I slide into my seat. "Guess what?" she asks.

"One of your YouTube videos went viral, and you're going to be whisked off to LA tomorrow."

"If only," she says. "But you know my new great friend Clarissa?"

"You mean your Tumblr mutual?"

She waves her hand. "Same thing. Anyways, she liked my post about the gig we're playing and then said"—Sook reads from her phone—"'Sounds cool. I'll be in town. See you there.' Can you believe it? Clarissa! Clarissa of Carousels! At our show!"

We have a gig coming up at a café known for its live music. It's a small spot, but they always feature great new bands, so it's pretty awesome they asked Dizzy Daisies to play. Sook said talent agents are even rumored to drop by sometimes.

"I can definitely believe it. Your music is great, and so are you."

Sook grins, then scoots forward. "I think I'm actually nervous. Thank god we have practice tonight. You didn't forget, did you?"

I had, in fact, forgotten.

Crap. Dinner at Amir's. Practice. And then this pile of homework. I pinch the bridge of my nose. "Of course not. What time again?"

"Hmm, think you can be over by seven?"

"I'll do my best."

"Thank you, really." Sook meets my eyes. "You're an awesome friend, Ariel."

The bell rings. Mrs. Rainer walks into the room jingling. There are little bells on the fringe of her scarf. I try and fail to bite back a yawn. I'm already tired at the thought of being tired.

We go over college essays again. I pull out my phone and

put a double asterisk next to mine on my to-do list. I've really got to get that done.

At the end of class, Mrs. Rainer hands back our *Crime and Punishment* essay tests. I'm always nervous turning over a grade, even for a class with an assured A. I take a tight breath and flip over my paper.

Seventy-eight.

I got a C.

But everyone told me this is the easiest AP class ever.

I grip the edge of my desk, pulse thudding in my ears as the bells rings. This isn't right. This can't be right. I brought up my calculus grade. Everything was supposed to be okay now.

"Ariel, coming?" Sook asks. She slips her purse over her shoulder. Her essay sits on top of her desk. Ninety-two. She barely studies anymore, devoting all her free time to the band, and she got a ninety-two.

For a moment, I hate my best friend.

"Uh, yeah, I'll be there soon. I've got to check some emails."

"Okay." She grabs her books and leaves.

I slide my phone out of my pocket and stare at the screen, waiting for the room to clear. My vision blurs. I rub my eyes hard.

Finally, it's Mrs. Rainer and me.

I walk over to her desk, shoving a shaking hand in my pocket. She slips off her reading glasses. They dangle on a chain around her neck. "Ariel, I'm glad you stayed. Let's talk."

"Is this…" My voice falters. "Is this graded right?"

I feel ridiculous asking the question, but I have to. I've found mistakes in the past, debated my way through unclear multiple-choice questions and exceptions of grammatical rules. Sometimes the A doesn't start as an A. Sometimes you have to argue your way up from a lower grade. Teachers here are used to it. Maybe there's room to negotiate.

"Ariel," Mrs. Rainer sighs. "This isn't a difficult class. I don't *want* to teach a difficult class. But to understand literature, one needs to read and participate. It's obvious you didn't finish the book."

I did. Okay, I didn't. I read most of the book. And the SparkNotes. Though switching back and forth between reading and audio did get a bit confusing. Still, I read more than enough to write a competent essay. "I read it," I lie. "I promise."

"Not closely, then. And you never participate in class conversation. You barely listen. You were on your phone again today! And it shows in your essay. This isn't some blow-off class. English is an integral part of everyone's future. If you can't read and write competently, you won't get anywhere."

I bite back the fact that I got a perfect verbal score on the SAT. "I'm sorry," I say. "It's been a difficult start to the semester, but I care about this class. I love English. Is there anything I can do? Rewrite the essay? Any extra credit?"

I practically hold my breath waiting for her to answer.

Finally Mrs. Rainer says, "I want you to succeed, Ariel. So I'll help you out. But promise you'll dedicate yourself to this extra work, not rush through it for the credit."

"I promise."

Relief sweeps through me. I push hair out of my eyes.

"All right." She grabs a thick book from her desk. It must be at least five hundred pages. "This is one of my favorite contemporary novels. It was published last year, so I doubt you'll find summaries and study guides online. Read it and pick another twenty-first-century novel, and then I want a twenty-page comparison essay."

My stomach lurches. "Twenty pages?"

Our final paper for the class is only fifteen.

"I'm trying to prepare you for college," Mrs. Rainer says. "You'll be writing essays that long for your courses there. And if this class is important to you, you'll make time."

Make time.

My vision blurs again.

I'm already taking six AP classes, sacrificing lunch, a full night's sleep, and a normal social life, so sure, I'll just *make time*.

"Do you want the extra credit or not?" Mrs. Rainer asks.

"I—" My voice catches. "Yes, I do. How much will it be worth?"

Mrs. Rainer sighs. "All about the grades." Well, fucking obviously. "If I find the essay satisfactory, I'll add five points to your final grade. All right?"

Five points. That's good at least.

"And don't dawdle with it," she continues. "I expect it on my desk within a couple of weeks."

"Absolutely. Thank you."

I leave and head straight to the bathroom. It's the old one, with a broken stall door and cracked mirrors, always empty. I grip the sink and take a shaky breath. My heart beats too hard. The pressure behind my eyes builds.

"*Fuck!*" I slap the porcelain sink, hands ringing with pain.

Tears release, but only a few. They slide down my cheeks. My stomach constricts, and I take a sharp breath.

Then the warning bell blares.

I splash water on my face and go to my next class.

———————————

"Ready?" Pari asks me, as we tune our instruments.

Today I'm playing my solo for Dr. Whitmore. I'm already on a precipice with English, so if I also mess this up…

"Ready," I lie, then lift my violin and pull my bow across the A string.

Dr. Whitmore exits her office and strides to the front of the room. She nods at me. "Afternoon, Ariel," she says brusquely. "I hope you've found the solo agreeable."

I wonder if she can read the *I hate you* in my eyes.

Everyone sets their instruments. A harpist and an oboe

player are joining us today to play the prelude to my solo. Dr. Whitmore drops her baton, and we begin. My pulse beats quickly, but I keep the tempo and play in tune. The piece now memorized, I even lift my eyes to watch the baton and meet Dr. Whitmore's cold gaze. I count the time I have left until my solo begins. A few pages. One page. Only lines now.

The oboe plays its prelude into my solo, each note perfectly sung, and then the room goes quiet and—

I begin, bow swiping too fast across the string. But I regain control. I play each note with precision and continue to meet Dr. Whitmore's eyes. The measures slip by, and then, it's over.

I hold my breath, waiting for her to say, *again*.

But Dr. Whitmore keeps tempo, the baton throwing another downbeat, and we continue into the next section. No *again*. We're still playing. I did it. Dr. Whitmore glances my way, and for a wild moment I expect possibly even a smile, but my heart drops when I meet her callous stare.

For the rest of class, my shoulders are taut, fingers stiff. When the bell rings, Dr. Whitmore calls me into her office. I head back with trepidation.

"The solo, Ariel, was unsatisfactory," she says. "There was no feeling. It was mechanical. Continue to work on it. Try to find the heart of the piece. But in the meantime, I'm going to consider an alternate for first chair. You'll both perform for me in three weeks, and then I'll make my decision. Now grab Pari for me before she leaves class."

———————

My ears buzz as I stand in the parking lot, like there's a radio playing on the wrong frequency. A thick knot hardens in my throat. My foot jumps up and down, as my mind races with everything I need to get done.

I'm standing with Sook and Amir while we wait for the parking lot to clear. Most days we hang out for twenty minutes, instead of sitting in a jammed line of cars.

Pari and Isaac head toward us. "L'Shana Tova!" Isaac says. Pari doesn't meet my eyes. Good.

"Shana Tova," I reply, mouth dry. I clear my throat. "Have a good New Year?" We grew up going to the same Sunday school classes at our synagogue, but I don't see him at services often anymore.

"Eh, I went to class instead of shul." Isaac hitches his bag up onto his shoulder. "Couldn't miss a full day. But Mom made brisket for dinner, so it's a good New Year so far."

"Nice." I nod.

"Sorry about the solo," Pari says. "Dr. Whitmore is such a—" She breaks off. "I don't like saying that word. But anyway, I thought you played it fine. Great!" She corrects herself.

Is Pari sorry? This is the opportunity she's always wanted.

She can take first chair from me. I can already imagine the letter she'll send to Harvard: *Dear Admissions Board, I have an addendum to my earlier application. I am now first chair violin of the Etta Fields Philharmonic Orchestra...*

We can't both be first chair. I'll have to hold off on my application until we play against each other so I don't look like I'm lying to Harvard.

"What happened with the solo?" Amir asks. His camera is out, and he's fiddling with the lens.

Exhaustion presses down on me. "It's nothing," I say. "Just a tricky piece."

I stare Pari down, pleading she'll drop it. Her brow tenses for a moment, then she shifts back on her feet. "C'mon, Isaac. We should go, start tackling that homework. It never ends, does it?"

"I'm ready to end it," Sook replies. "I want out now. Hell, I wanted out last year."

It can't be that bad, I want to say. *You're only taking four AP classes, and your safety school is freaking Dartmouth.*

"We'll see you guys later." Isaac waves, and they walk toward his car.

Amir glances at me. "I'm going to leave also. I want to get some film developed. Ariel, want to hang after dinner? We can study." His smile is shy. "Or not study."

How do I tell the guy I like that I need to be alone? Sook

answers before I have to: "Sorry, lover boy, he's practicing with the band. We have a gig coming up, which *you* should come to."

"Already in my calendar," Amir replies. "What about tomorrow, Ariel?"

Tomorrow I'll be behind on the work I have to push aside tonight. My brain spins. There's too much to do. "I can't. I'm—" I glance between the two of them. "I have a lot of catch-up work from the holiday. I might be a little MIA for a few days."

"Unfortunate." Amir clicks the lens into place. He snaps a picture of Sook and me. "But if you must. I'll still see you at dinner." He steps forward and kisses me softly on the lips, but my thoughts are on all the work I have.

I lean back and bite my nail. "And I'll still see you at school."

"Yes, you will." He waves at Sook. "All right. Bye, guys. Have a good practice."

"Thank you!" Sook says, as he walks away. Then she turns to me. "He's quite cute."

I run a hand through my hair. "Yes, I agree."

"You *will* be at practice tonight, right?"

A sharp headache presses against my right temple. "Of course."

"*Ocean's Eight!*" Rasha shouts, then waves her hands. "No, wait! *Finding Dory?*"

"Yes!" Rachel squeals. She jumps forward and gives her a high-ten.

"They're competitive," I whisper to Amir. We're sitting on the love seat together as our family plays charades after dinner. I needed to leave five minutes ago for Dizzy Daisies practice, but it's rude to come to a Naeem family dinner and only stay for the food.

"I was going to say annoying," he responds.

We laugh. His eyes spark when they meet mine. In an alternate reality, it's been the perfect night. Mr. Naeem made my favorite, chicken karahi, a Pakistani curry dish that somehow tastes even better than it smells. Our parents didn't embarrass us at dinner; well, with the exception of Mrs. Naeem saying, "Ariel, will you pass the water to your boyfriend?"

Amir and I both blushed, but neither of us denied it, either, and that made me blush again, but in a nice way.

But now it's after dinner, and we're playing charades, and my mind is swimming with the to-do list in my phone, and I can't even begin to touch the work until after band practice.

"Amir, your turn!" my dad says. "Come on—the guys need redemption!"

Amir nudges me and raises his eyebrows. "Here we go."

"Good luck!" I say.

He gets up and pulls a scrap of paper from the bowl. His eyes flicker with recognition, and his shoulders relax. Good, it'll be a fast one, and since everyone will have gone once, I can make my exit after.

"And go!" Mrs. Naeem says. She leans back onto the couch, crossing one leg over the other. Her black motorcycle boots match Rasha's.

Amir boxes his hands together. "TV show!" I say.

He nods. Dad and Mr. Naeem lean forward. Next, Amir marches in place. "An army show," Mr. Naeem says. "What are some army shows?"

"What about—" Dad begins.

Amir shakes his head. Nope, not an army show. Next he stretches, reaching one arm over the top of his head at a time. His shirt lifts up, and I avert my eyes, because I don't need the embarrassment of my parents watching me watch Amir.

"Something with athletics?" Dad asks. "Sports television…"

Mrs. Naeem must have written the clue because she cups her hands together and whisper-shouts. "Try jumping jacks!"

Amir, distracted, pauses what he's doing. He shakes his head, trying to decide his next move. Mrs. Naeem leans over to Rasha and whispers something to her. Rasha laughs, then says, "Amir, next clue! They won't get it with that."

"What is it?" Mr. Naeem asks them. "Give us a hint!"

"No cheating!" Sara says.

"They started it!" her dad responds.

The timer buzzes. Amir's lips set into a firm line.

Mrs. Naeem winces. "Oh, I'm sorry, beta." She picks up her phone. "Here—you want more time? We won't talk."

Amir shakes his head and sits down next to me, sinking into the couch. "It's fine," he says. "Who's next?"

Mrs. Naeem looks truly sorry, and I want Amir to let her off the hook. But he's already staring at his phone, scrolling through a photo blog. Then, my alarm goes off.

"Crap," I mutter. "I need to head out."

Amir is quiet, retreated into himself. I don't want to leave him like this. But Sook needs me at practice. This gig is huge for her, and we have to prepare.

"Talk later tonight, okay?" I ask Amir.

He nods, still looking at his phone. So, I pull mine out and send him a message. A second later, his phone chimes. He looks at it and smiles, then nudges my side. I smile and nudge back.

As I get up to leave, my phone buzzes: *I ship us more than I ship Harry and Cedric too.*

TWELVE

By the end of the week, I'm exhausted, but I actually feel good, in control. Buckling down the last couple of days has been nice. Familiar. I get this weird high when I'm hyperproductive and always checking something off my list. And I have a lot on my list.

I planned out all of my classwork by the hour. So if I pull an all-nighter tonight and only sleep for five hours a night going forward, I'll be back on track within a week. Maybe four hours a night. But it'll be fine. I can sleep when I graduate.

As we sit down for Shabbat dinner, I have the giant novel Mrs. Rainer gave me to read in my lap. I'll finish it tonight and pick out a comp book this weekend. Mom recites the prayer for the candles and joins us at the table.

"Ariel, Rachel, books away," Dad says, raising the wineglass.

I glance in Rachel's direction. She's reading a book that looks heavier than mine.

"One second," I respond, scanning the rest of my page, then shutting the novel and looking up.

Rachel's still bent over her book. She's twists a piece of her hair, round and round, tight around her finger. "Book away, Rachel," Dad repeats.

"I'm not hungry," she says.

"*Ra-chell*," Dad warns. He pulls out the Hebrew pronunciation, so he means business.

Rachel sighs loudly and slams her book closed. "Fine, whatever."

"What is that?" I ask.

"An encyclopedia," she tells me.

"But…internet…" I say.

"They want us to cite sources." She groans. "I don't know. It's so old. And boring. It's about weather."

"What's the assignment?" Mom asks.

"It's nothing. Boring. Next topic."

Mom hesitates, raising an eyebrow at Dad, but moves on. "What about you, boychik? Good book?"

"It's fine. For school."

"We couldn't keep you away from the library when you were Rachel's age," Dad says. "Maybe you should ease back on some of that work. Read something for fun."

I give him a weak smile. "Yeah."

I don't get my parents. They brag about me applying to Harvard, but then they nag me for working too hard. They don't understand, I guess. They *can't* understand. Harvard demands perfection. So many of these schools demand perfection. And I'm not like my parents. Perfection isn't natural for me—I have to make sacrifices.

We say the prayer for the wine and challah and dig into dinner, but I can't concentrate on conversation. There's still so much to do. Our game of bloopers and highlights goes by in record time, Rachel and I giving short answers. As I butter my end-of-meal third slice of challah, Rachel asks, "May I be excused?" Her plate is already empty, and she's kicking her legs against the chair.

Mom and Dad have another silent exchange. "We were thinking we could go for ice cream after dinner. What do you guys think?"

"Awesome," Rachel says. "Bring me back some, please. Mint chocolate chip!"

She scampers upstairs. Dad sighs. "What about you, Ariel?"

I know it's a jerk move, but I also pretend to not get their point. "Mint chocolate chip sounds great." I stand up and grab my book. "Thanks, guys. Have fun!"

At least I can read this absurdly long book from bed. I prop it up with a pillow on my stomach. My window is cracked open, so the brisk October wind blows into my room, while my speakers play the Grateful Dead's "Touch of Grey."

It's late, almost one in the morning, and I'm reading by the light of my lamp. The book isn't bad. It's just long. Three hundred pages is enough for me to get the gist, but it keeps going and going. I yawn, then take a sip of the Coke next to me. It's getting warm, but the ice machine is loud, and I don't want to wake anyone up. I grab a bag of Sour Patch Kids off my nightstand and eat them two at a time.

Next door the floor creaks. Is Rachel awake? I wait a moment, and the house settles. I pick up my phone and see a message from Sook: *Adding a practice tomorrow. What time works for you?*

I groan. I'm tempted to text back and say, *I'm sorry, Sook, I can't do this. I have too much work and not enough time.* But this gig is so important to her. So I text back: *4 but I can only do a couple hours*

Sook: *Okay thank you love you*

I was hoping to squeeze in time to see Amir tomorrow, but that's going to have to wait until Sunday. Besides, I don't need him seeing me this stressed. I probably already weirded him out with my math panic. He can't see me at Peak Ariel.

I yawn, eyes blinking closed. No. Can't sleep.

I take another swig of Coke and keep reading.

———

"Coffee anyone?" I ask, thudding downstairs to Sook's basement. It's Saturday afternoon. This morning I practically sleepwalked through services and my shift at the animal shelter. I was in such a daze, I almost forgot to put three of the dogs back in their cages before leaving. At Dunkin' Donuts, I asked for a double shot in my coffee.

"Oh my god, yes please." Malka gratefully accepts a cup.

"I'm good," Sook says.

"Cool, I'll drink yours." My phone buzzes, telling me it's time for practice to start. My pulse races, and my leg shakes up and down. Maybe I didn't need a double shot after drinking coffee at both Kiddush and the shelter. "Y'all ready to play? I have to head out at six."

"Oooh," Sook says. "Going out on a date with Amir?"

"Nah, dinner with the family."

And then I'll be up late working. I allotted myself five hours of sleep tonight, but this caffeine might keep me awake until dawn. Good. Maybe I'll get ahead.

We set up our instruments and start a new song. It's a small set, but Sook pleaded until I agreed to play five full songs with them instead of just the couple I remember signing up for. The violin interludes are easy, but each note is painful. To keep first chair, I'm practicing constantly. Calluses can't form soon enough.

My mind drifts to my to-do list as Sook and Malka pause to discuss song order. In my rush to make up points in English, I forgot I have to read a thirty-page short story for Spanish lit and also take an online quiz for AP Psychology. Weirdly, calculus is now one of the few classes I'm not worried about. Studying with Amir has set me on the right track with the material, and I've gotten used to Mr. Eller's haphazard teaching style.

Practice continues. This session is supposed to have us ready for the gig. But even though I play each note right, we don't fit together yet. As much as I plan and prepare, nothing seems to go right.

The next morning, I climb out of the shower yawning. I rub the fogged-up mirror to see red eyes. "Crap," I mutter and then move around stuff in my junk drawer until I find my Visine. I squeeze two drops in each eye and blink.

Yesterday, my alarm buzzed at six, and I told the girls I had to leave, but our sound still wasn't right. I reasoned it was better to get the practice over with than have Sook asking me to come back again, so I stuck with it until we blended together seamlessly.

But then I didn't get home until nine and stayed up until five in the morning finishing that damn book. My sleep after that was short and fitful, body still buzzing from caffeine.

I've got to get some sleep before school tomorrow. Maybe even sneak in time for a run. At least there's no zero period this year. Last year, Sook picked me up during pitch-black winter mornings to make it to school on time for zero period health class. The year before that, Mom drove me in early for AP Latin.

I crack another giant yawn and force myself out of the bathroom. Rachel's soccer game starts soon, and no matter my workload, I can't miss it.

Twenty minutes later, I'm parked and walking down to the field. I scroll through my phone, looking at popular twenty-first-century novels and trying to find a short one that will work. But not so short that Mrs. Rainer will suspect I'm cutting corners.

"Ariel."

"Hmm?" I didn't realize I'd gotten so close to where everyone is standing. Amir is right in front of me. It's been days since I've seen him outside of school. It's like my brain put him in this other compartment, but now I'm inhaling spearmint and basil, and I'm so damn tired, I just want to put my head on his shoulder and have him wrap his arms around me.

Instead, I yawn. "Hey."

"Hey, sleepy." He smiles, and my stomach flip-flops. "I missed you."

I'm too tired to subdue my unruly grin. "Missed you too. Sorry I'm so busy."

"It's okay. You warned me. How's English going?"

I shrug. "Getting there. It's a ridiculous amount of extra

work. Between that and Spanish lit, I never want to read another book again."

"Except Harry Potter," Amir says.

I laugh. "Except Harry Potter." I glance at our families, talking and gathered around the food as always. "I should probably go say hi to everyone."

Amir tsks. "You're probably right."

We chat with our parents and Rasha as the game starts. It's kind of nice. As we get into the first half, my phone buzzes, reminding me to go to the bookstore after the game. I need to pick out a novel now so I can be in and out when I get to the store.

Amir is talking with Rasha, so I head down the sideline and scroll through books again. The sun beats down through scattered clouds. I sit in the grass and hunch over my phone, tapping my calendar. The Harvard application date looms closer. I click my screen off and try to force away the thought. Then before I know it, my eyes dip shut. I don't fall asleep, but I'm in some half state, the sounds of the game in the far background.

"You okay?" Amir asks.

My eyes are slow to open. I focus on him, having to squint. "Hmm, yeah. A little tired." I pat the grass next to me. "Come sit. It's so nice out."

Amir hesitates, like he wants to say something else, but then he sits close enough that his shoulder presses against mine.

His touch steadies me. I lean into him, and my eyes blink closed.

"You missed a goal," Amir says.

"Rachel or Sara?"

"The other team."

I wince. "Bummer. They'll get it back." I pick up a piece of grass and shred it with my fingers. Amir does the same. "So what's going on with you?" I ask. "How was the rest of your week?"

"Well…"

I glance over, and Amir is smiling one of the biggest smiles I've ever seen from him. It's an Ariel-sized smile, but he doesn't try to hide it. I perk up a bit and lean forward. "Tell me."

"You know that art show I was applying to? The one with the scholarship?" I nod. "I got in!"

"Holy shit, Amir. That's amazing. Congrats!"

Without thinking, I lean forward and kiss him quick across the lips. He kisses me back, softer and longer, and I melt against his touch. God, I missed him.

"Thank you," he says, nudging into my shoulder. "For the congrats and the kiss. It's this Friday. Will you come?"

I stay smiling, but beneath the surface, my pulse races. Of course, I want to go, but will I have caught up on enough work by then? I can't keep adding things to my schedule and expect to get it all done. The gig Saturday night is already going to devour a large part of next weekend. This is why I never date during the school year.

But being with Amir seemed more like an inevitability than a choice.

Amir looks hopeful, happy. This is huge for him. "Of course I'll be there."

Eager shouts erupt from the sidelines. We look to the field and watch as Rachel scores a goal.

"Told you they'd get it back," I say.

"She'd make a great chaser."

"Does everything relate to Harry Potter in your mind?"

"Hey, don't knock it. What's so bad about seeing magic everywhere?"

"You're right." I lean against him again, my body at ease. "Nothing wrong with a little magic."

THIRTEEN

"All right, everyone. You may get started. Feel free to brainstorm with your classmates," Mrs. Chen says.

I grip my pencil and try to concentrate, but my eyes won't focus. A vicious headache beats against my skull. I should've packed more than a granola bar, or made time to run by the cafeteria for a slice of pizza. I need sleep, and if not, calories. Covertly, I sneak a sip of my energy drink under the table.

We're supposed to make up our own government and map out the power structure. At least it's only a completion grade.

I feel Pari's stare on me. "Are you okay, Ariel?"

"Yeah, fine."

"You can talk to me, you know," she says. "Whatever it is."

She probably means it. Probably.

But my interior is already cracking. I can't let my exterior fall apart also. Soon we'll both play the Rimsky-Korsakov solo. If I show weakness now, she'll know she has a chance to steal my chair and practice harder to do so.

"It's nothing." I twist my pencil. "A busy week. I'm fine."

"I know it's hard, but keep perspective. None of this will matter in a year."

"Really?" Hostility edges into my tone. "You really think this won't matter?"

"It's only high school. I've been telling myself this for months. I still don't always believe it, but it's true. We'll graduate and go to college, and none of this will matter."

Every muscle stiffens, prepared for flight or—

"It all matters, Pari. Don't be ridiculous."

She opens her mouth, then shuts it. Her eyes shine. When she speaks, her choked voice cuts into me. "I'm not being *ridiculous.*"

The energy drink churns in my stomach. I shouldn't have said that. I start to apologize when she continues, "You can be a jerk, Ariel. I've worked as hard as you. I'm as smart. You think I'm ridiculous, why? Because you found the online AP class and I didn't? Congratulations. That definitely makes you better than me." She clenches her jaw. "I was trying to help you, but I guess you're fine on your own. Good luck. I hope you end up with everything you think is so important."

She turns away from me and leans over her paper, hair falling to block her face.

I go back to my empty page.

I wince as I button my shirt. It's Wednesday morning and Yom Kippur, the holiest day of the year, so I'll be at services instead of school. My fingers are tender with new blisters. Last night I skipped my family's annual tradition of pizza dinner before fasting for Yom Kippur because Sook called for an extra emergency practice. Then I was about to go to sleep at two in the morning, when I remembered I had to email my Spanish teacher a short story analysis since I'd be missing the in-class quiz.

By the time I crawled into bed, the sun was threatening to come up, and then the wink of sleep I did get was filled with stress dreams, snatches of Mrs. Rainer lecturing me and Pari's eyes filling with tears. She doesn't get how difficult this is for me, but still, I shouldn't have treated her like that. I owe her an apology.

My stomach growls as I walk into synagogue. My family is already here. I took my own car since I was running late. There are hundreds of people streaming in and milling around the lobby. My stomach growls louder, but the noise covers it. I think I might have only had lunch yesterday, a rushed turkey sandwich between classes. Not a smart move the day before fasting for Yom Kippur.

I find my parents standing near the sanctuary doors. Rachel usually skips off to say hi to her friends, but today she's glued to our parents' sides. "How was pizza last night?" I ask her.

"Fine."

I gnaw a hangnail. She seems down. "You going to the animal shelter with me next weekend? Ezekiel misses you."

Rachel gives a half smile. "I miss him too. I'll come."

I knock into her shoulder lightly. "Good."

We head into services, bodies pressing around us. I falter a step, feeling light-headed and overwhelmed by the crowd. We make it inside and sit on folding chairs near the back of the shul. Sitting feels good. I run my hand through my hair before pinning my kippah. My fingers fumble with the bobby pin.

My phone buzzes. Malka: *Where are you?*

I reply: *Near the back. Folding chairs. You?*

Malka: *Benches on the left. Parents aren't going to stay the whole time. Can you give me a ride home after?*

I text back: *Sure*

I check my to-do list for the rest of the week. I should reassess, break the work down by the hour again, but I'm worried if I do, I'll realize I don't have enough time to get it all done. At least I finished reading both the books for English. Now I just have to write the paper.

Just write a twenty-page paper.

I laugh, almost delirious. Dad glances at me, but I stare down at my siddur.

Services go by in a daze. There's so much standing and sitting, when all I want to do is lie down. It's the longest service of the year, and doesn't end until past three. "I'll see y'all at home," I tell my parents. "I'm giving Malka a ride."

"Okay, tatala," Mom says.

I slip out quickly before most people stand up. I don't have the energy to schmooze today.

I walk down to the east wing of the synagogue. Malka texts that she's caught in the Jewish goodbye vortex and will escape as soon as she can. So that means it'll be at least thirty minutes.

The hallway is blissfully deserted. There's a couch outside Rabbi Solomon's office. I sink into it, then curl up on my side. Might as well hang out here and be comfortable until Malka is ready.

I yawn a tiny yawn. It reminds me of Pari. I really should apologize…

"Ariel?"

My eyes blink open.

Rabbi Solomon stands over me, hands on her hips, looking concerned. "Are you all right?"

I clear my throat and slide to a sitting position. Too fast. I hold my head and close my eyes, waiting for the dizzy feeling to go away. *I'm a dizzy daisy.* I laugh out loud.

"Can you stand? Come into my office."

"I should…"

She waves off my nonexcuse. "For a minute. Come now."

I stand slowly then take a short breath and follow her inside. "Sit," she says. She reaches into a drawer and pulls out a white baker's box. There are a dozen pieces of mandel bread inside. "Here, eat. I'm going to grab you a cup of water."

My rabbi is handing me food on Yom Kippur.

"But I'm fasting…"

"Hashem understands. You need nourishment."

I hesitate, but grab a piece of mandel bread. I'm already starting on my second by the time Rabbi Solomon comes back with a cup of water.

"What's going on, Ariel?" she asks. "Are you sick? Have you been sleeping well?"

I hesitate. Lying to a rabbi seems real un-kosher.

Rabbi Solomon answers the silence. "Perhaps I should go find your parents. Tell them you're not feeling well."

"That's really not necessary," I say a bit too loudly. Mom has a filing deadline for a story tomorrow night, and Dad is in court all next week. I don't need to bother them over nothing. "Really," I say. "I'm good."

"How about this then—you call me after the holiday and make a time to come see me. We'll have a little chat. You'll be off to college before we know it."

"And you won't talk to my parents?"

"If you come here and chat with me, then no, I won't talk to your parents."

"Okay, sure," I reply, head throbbing. One more thing on my list. "I'll be here."

"Thanks for the ride," Malka says.

My fingers tap the steering wheel. Why won't this car in front of me move? *Move!* The parking lot is gridlocked. I need to get home. I thought I'd be there almost an hour ago, but time is slipping away. I need a plan. Okay, first I'll start the paper—

"Ariel, you can go," Malka says as the car behind me honks.

I startle and press my foot to the gas. The car jerks forward. "Crap, sorry," I mutter. I put on my blinker and turn out of the parking lot.

Okay, so first I'll start the paper, and then I'll take a break and work through the practice problems for—

"Um, Ariel? My house is the other way."

I glance at Malka, then back at the road. "Right. Sorry." I was on autopilot thinking about getting home. The light in front of me turns yellow, but the lanes are clear, so I press down on the gas and whip a U-turn to take us back toward Malka's house.

"Whoa, there," she says, touching the roof of the car. "Okay, fast and furious."

"What?"

She gives me a funny look. "Nothing. Speaking of fast, how's yours going?"

My stomach growls. The mandel bread only made me hungrier. Screw it. I should eat when I get home. If the rabbi says I can eat, then I can eat, right? I'll get home and have a nosh, and then I'll start the paper, and then I'll take a break and work through the practice problems for—

"Ariel!" Malka shouts.

A car horn blares behind me as I finish crossing an intersection. I glance in my rearview mirror. A car coming from the cross street is stalled in the middle of the road. Wait, what just happened?

Malka is gripping the *oh shit* handle. "The light was *red*," she says, voice taut. "Slow down. Please slow down."

My heart can't slow down. It's racing a hundred miles an hour, like someone cut the brakes. My mind swims with exhaustion. "*Sorry*," I say, but my voice isn't even a whisper. I clear my throat. "Sorry, sorry."

"We're almost there. Please be careful."

I can feel Malka's tense muscles, body bracing for an accident. Shit. *Shit.*

I place both hands on the wheel and stare at the road. *Focus, Ariel. Drive down the street. Take a right into Malka's neighborhood. Slow, now. Twenty-five miles an hour. Make it twenty. Pull into her driveway. Car in park. You're on a hill. Emergency brake.*

Malka puts her hand on mine. I'm still gripping the wheel. I don't want to look at her. I *can't* look at her.

"Ariel, you want to come in for a little bit? We can take a Yom Kippur catnap."

I blink. A nap would be nice. But I'm already late. I'll get home and have a nosh, and then I'll start the paper—

"Ariel?"

I turn to her and force a smile. "Nah, I'm good," I say. My hand shakes, so I grip the wheel tighter. "I'm not tired."

FOURTEEN

"Pizza or mac and cheese?" I ask Rachel.

"Um, mac and cheese?" she responds from the living room floor, where she's surrounded by puffy paint and poster board and pictures of pirates.

"You got it."

I made it to the end of the week. I turned in the massive English paper, caught up on my Spanish reading, and snagged another A on a calculus quiz. Our parents are out for Shabbat dinner at a friend's house, so I'm cooking for Rachel, stirring while reading notes for AP Gov on my phone.

My phone rings. It's Malka. *Calling* me. I've been brushing off her texts since Yom Kippur, quick responses like "all good" and "awesome." I'm tempted to ignore her, but I answer the call.

"*Hey!*" I say, voice too bright.

"*Hey,*" she says, suspicious of my too-bright voice.

I stir the mac and cheese. "Shabbat Shalom."

"Shabbat Shalom. So, what are you up to tonight?"

This isn't normal. We both know this isn't normal. We don't call—we text. I shift on my feet before answering. "Making some dinner for Rachel. Parents are out, so we're going to hang here." The line buzzes. Should I invite her over? No, I have too much work to do. "What about you?"

"I'm—" She pauses. "Look, Ariel, are you okay? You really freaked me out on Yom Kippur."

My pulse races. "I'm great. Fine."

"You were really distracted and—"

"I was *fasting*," I say. "I was hungry. It's all good. I promise."

The line buzzes again. "Do you maybe want to—"

"Ah! Water's boiling over. Sorry, got to go!"

I hang up the phone, then turn it on silent. If I can't hear her calling, then I can't stress about whether or not to pick up. Running a red light was not good, but I know that. I don't need her worrying about it. I'll be better, get more sleep. In fact, after practicing my solo tonight, I'm planning on getting a solid eight hours. It's fine.

I'm fine.

When the food is ready, I call Rachel to the table. "Can we eat in here?" Rachel asks. "I want to keep working."

"Sure." I carry the bowls into the family room and settle on the couch. I can read over more notes while eating, then practice violin for a few hours, and still be asleep by midnight.

Rachel and I both demolish our mac and cheese, then continue to work. Squeaking markers, cutting paper, rustling pages, the sounds are nice ambience as I study. Every now and then Rachel glances back for my opinion. "Do you like that?" she asks, after pasting a close-up of a sword next to a full illustration of her pirate.

"Awesome, good choice."

I ask if she wants ice cream before I go upstairs, and she says yes and joins me in the kitchen to make it. We go for full sundaes, whipped cream, cherries, and all.

"What are you working on?" She twirls her spoon in the ice cream but doesn't eat it.

I sigh. "Like, everything. When is your pirate project due?"

"Next week." She stares at her untouched dessert.

"Aren't you going to eat any?"

She twists her mouth. "Put it in the freezer for me? My stomach feels kind of funny. Too much mac."

"Sure," I say.

She hugs me with one arm, her body warm and close, before retreating to the living room. I put her ice cream in the freezer, but only after stealing a bite.

———————

I clean the dishes and check on Rachel before heading upstairs. She's still at work on her project, but she has the Disney Channel on in the background.

Up in my room, I crack my knuckles, then examine the pads of my fingers, half-callused and half-blistered, already aggravated from doing the dishes. But I have to practice. Less than two weeks until I play the solo against Pari.

I can picture her, playing with intent, hair swept back into a sleek ponytail, fingernails coated with cracked blue polish, conjuring each note with heartfelt perfection. If Harvard has two applicants from Etta Fields High School, will they take first chair or second?

I grab a couple Band-Aids from the bathroom and wrap them around the worst of my fingers. Then I lift my violin and begin to tune it, turning the small metal screws. "Shit!" I gasp, fingers burning, almost dropping the instrument. Tears spring to my eyes.

How am I supposed to do this? I have to practice the solo to keep first chair. I'm nowhere near ready. But the gig with Dizzy Daisies is tomorrow night, and Sook wants a full dress rehearsal beforehand.

My fingers throb. I can't do this. I physically can't keep this up. I can push my mind all I want, but my skin will crack and bleed. I wipe away more tears as they come.

Try again. It's not that bad. I'll play through the solo, see how it goes.

I lift my violin and grimace as I place my fingers on the strings. Tears spring up again. Ignore them. I begin to play, pain vibrating through me. I try to zone out and sink into the music, think only of the notes and their arrangement. And it works. I make it through. But when I'm done, the pain rushes back, and there's blood on my strings.

"Fuck." My heart drops. Just do it. Get it over with.

I wipe my bloody fingers on my jeans and then text Sook: *I'm so sorry. I can't play with you guys tomorrow night.*

I stare at the message, weary and numb. What kind of a best friend bails at the last minute, especially on something so important?

A moment later, Sook is calling me.

I swallow hard, pulse racing, then tap ignore and turn off my phone. It seems safer than silent.

I'll go to sleep, rest my mind and fingers, and get back to work tomorrow. Everything will be better in the morning. I strip down to my boxers and climb into bed, pulling the comforter over me. It's warm and safe and dark. My body sinks into the mattress. The second my eyes dip closed, I'm asleep.

I wake up to darkness and frantic voices. Disoriented, I roll over to check the time, but my phone is off. My laptop is on the floor by my bed. I open it and see it's little past four in the morning. My head is swimming, jarred from heavy sleep.

The voices are too muffled to hear. I throw off my covers, get up, and crack open my door. The hallway is bright. Half of the house lights are on.

I head downstairs. Mom is in the kitchen, pulling on a jacket over her sleep shirt and pajama pants. Dad is pacing in the living room, on the phone. "Yes, we're on our way. Bringing her now."

"What's going on?" I ask.

Then I hear it. Rachel. Her cry sounds more animal than human. I rush into the living room. Her project supplies are still out on the floor, and she's on the couch, clutching her stomach, tears streaming down her cheeks.

My pulse thuds in my ears. "What is it?" I turn to my parents. "What's going on?"

"We don't know," Dad says, getting off the phone. "C'mon. We're going to the hospital."

"Okay, um, I'll put clothes on."

I rush upstairs, almost tripping on a step, then yank a shirt on and pull sweatpants over my boxers. When I get to the garage, my parents are already piling Rachel in the car. She's quieter, whimpering. Maybe it's her appendix? Or something she ate? Was it the mac and cheese?

But then I'd be sick, too.

I slide in next to her and sit in the middle seat so I can keep my arm around her. "I'm sorry, I'm sorry, I'm sorry," I say, even though I have no idea what I'm sorry for.

Dad walks into the waiting room. "No update yet," he says.

Rachel was admitted into the ER two hours ago. They've ruled out imminently life-threatening diagnoses, but that's of little comfort since they still don't know what's going on.

"How's she feeling?"

"Better, Baruch Hashem. They gave her some pain and anxiety medication, but since we don't know what caused the symptoms…"

Dad trails off and kind of blank stares at the wall. It's unsettling to see him like this. Dad is always in control, but in this moment he looks as lost as I feel. I stand and wrap my arms around him. He's still taller than me. I tuck my head against his shoulder, and he hugs me back. I close my eyes and breathe deep, and for a moment I feel safe, protected, like a kid again. "I love you," I say.

"Love you, too, Ariel." We stay like that for a while until Dad steps away, running a hand through his hair, the curls wilder than usual. "I'm going to get more coffee. Do you want anything?"

"Coffee sounds good."

I rub my eyes and settle back into my chair, both wired and exhausted. It's strange to sit here with nothing to do. I never sit still, never hit pause. Restlessness makes my skin crawl.

I have my phone, but I'm nervous to turn it on and see messages from Sook.

The waiting room is mostly empty. There's an elderly

couple who look like they've been camped out all day. A young family with multiple little kids wanting to be entertained. A girl with torn jeans and a hoodie sitting alone.

I glance down to see what they see. A teenage guy with curly hair, wearing black sweatpants and a Led Zeppelin T-shirt.

After ten minutes pass, Dad still isn't back, and my nerves kick into overdrive.

I don't understand what happened.

I don't understand what's happening.

My leg shakes up and down. I need to do *something*. Sighing, I turn on my phone.

Texts from Sook light up the screen. The most recent one begins: *I can't believe you would...*

The gnawing guilt I felt only hours ago is now tucked far away. I think my brain is compartmentalizing because I can only deal with so much stress at once. I scroll past her texts and find some from Amir. I've barely seen him all week, and my body actually aches to have him near me. Feeling a trace of relief, I open the thread and read:

Hey what time are you coming?

Are you on the way?

I'm in the back left corner

There's only an hour left

I hope you're okay

...Thanks for the support

I blink. Oh. Oh. *Fuck.* It takes all my willpower not to throw my phone across the room. I forgot about Amir's photography show. I set an alarm to remind me earlier this week, but then I was so distracted with all my work, and then I turned off my phone...

I glance at the time. It's six thirty on a Saturday morning. My weekend plans had been set. Amir's photography show on Friday. Gig with Dizzy Daisies on Saturday. But then I chose my work over them. And now my sister is in the freaking ER, and I'm alone in the waiting room, having fucked up my relationships with the few close friends I have.

I can't deal with this. I *can't.*

I'm about to turn off my phone again, when it starts ringing. Startled, I almost drop it. Amir is calling. But I didn't text him back...

I pick up. "Hello?"

"Ariel." His warm voice stirs unexpected emotions. My eyes blur. I close them and pinch the bridge of my nose. *Breathe.* "I'm so sorry," he says. "I just heard about Rachel. My mom is about to leave for the hospital. Want me to come with her? I can bring sour gummy worms."

Oh, of course. My mom probably texted Mrs. Naeem. They're so close. "Um, that's okay...I mean...maybe later. I don't know what's happening yet."

"All right, whatever you want. No pressure at all."

It's weird to talk on the phone with him. He sounds so distant.

"I'm sorry," he says. "For all the texts. I had no idea what was happening with Rachel. I must have sounded so callous."

"Oh," I say. "Yeah, she was fine then, um…"

Silence.

"What?"

"She was fine earlier. I forgot about your show. I'm really sorry, Amir. I had a reminder on my phone, but I turned off my phone because I've been really stressed with school…"

"Oh," he says.

"I'm really sorry."

"I don't want to be mad at you right now." His voice is tight, words measured. "Your sister is in the hospital."

"But you are mad at me."

"I'm—it was important."

More silence. I clear my throat. "How did it go?"

"Yeah, I don't think…let's not do that. I'm here if you need me later, okay?" He sounds like he wants to hang up.

"Okay," I say.

I keep the phone pressed to my ear, wondering if he'll say anything else, but then the line goes silent.

Around nine in the morning, they moved Rachel from the ER into a regular room. The second I got there, I ran in and hugged her, lump in my throat. She looked tiny in the bed—young. She's a kid. She's only a kid. I feel like I'm not the only one who forgets that.

Now it's almost noon. Rachel and I both dozed for a while, but it's hard to sleep with the beeping machines and nurses hustling in and out, so we've been playing Scrabble on my phone while our parents step out of the room to call family members with updates.

"Don't do it," I warn. Normally, I don't *let* Rachel win. She's too smart and beats me plenty on her own, but I couldn't help but leave a triple word score open for her today. She's alert and cheerful considering, her pain mostly gone, but the color is still drained from her cheeks. I hate not knowing what caused this.

"I'm doing it." She grins and puts down the word: *Jinx*.

I groan. "You're killing me."

Rachel smiles, but it doesn't quite reach her eyes. "*You* picked the game. Your turn."

I'm taking the phone back when the doctor walks into the room. She's wearing scrubs and sneakers. My parents follow her in. We all stare at the doctor, waiting for her to say something.

Rachel speaks first. "So," she says. "What's wrong with me?"

She asks it in such a perfunctory way, we all laugh, breaking some of the tension in the room. "Well, let's see if your brother will wait outside," the doctor replies.

"That's okay," Rachel says. "I want him in here."

Why would the doctor want me to wait outside?

"Yeah." I cross my arms. "I'm good here."

Mom and Dad nod also.

"All right," the doctor says. "So, good news first: all of your CT scans were clear. We're still waiting on some blood work, but our best guess is you had a psychosomatic response last night, which manifested as sharp abdominal pains."

"Wait," Dad says. "What?"

"In layman's terms," the doctor continues, "she was upset, and it caused physical pains. It's common for stress to lead to this sort of reaction."

"Stress?" Mom rubs her forehead. "What do you mean—"

"Is she okay now?" Dad asks. "I don't understand."

"Of course she's not okay," Mom snaps. She then softens her voice. "It's not physical, but that doesn't mean it's not harmful."

"Right, no, of course," Dad says.

I'm sitting there trying to take in all of the information, but the pieces don't fit together. "Stress?" I ask. "She's ten. What caused…"

I think of last night and the pirate project spread out all over the floor. I think of the last few weeks and Rachel doing homework instead of playing with the animals at the shelter, not putting her book down at the table. I turn to my sister.

"Rachel…" I start, not wanting to say it. "Are you stressed about your project? Is it school?"

Her face is still hard. Then, it crumples. Her voice cracks when she speaks. "I just wanted to do a good job."

She starts crying, and I try to fight back my own tears. I want to escape, but this is my sister. I need to be here for her. So, I move to her bed and hug her. She buries her face in my shoulder, and I bury my face in her pillow, and we both let the tears come.

He's standing in front of the cages, finger looped through the bars, varsity jacket thrown over his shoulder. "Isaac?" I ask.

He turns and blinks. The animal shelter is busy today. There's a family and a single guy up front, both waiting to sign adoption papers with Marnie. So Isaac and I are back here all alone. I don't think either of us expected to run into anyone.

"Hey, sorry," he says. "The woman, um, Marnie, said I could come back here." His eyes are unfocused, hair unkempt. "I'm supposed to be at practice…" He lets the sentence hang without further explanation. "What about you?"

"Uh." My brain freezes. Then, the truth. "I just got back from the hospital. My sister is sick."

"Oh damn, is she going to be okay? What is it? The flu?"

"No." I scratch the back of my neck. "Stress. Uh, school stress."

"It made her sick?"

I nod. "Guess so."

My throat constricts thinking about it. My little sister was in the hospital—the *freaking hospital*—because of school. And Malka and I could've landed there when I was driving her home the other day. Because of school.

"That's messed up," Isaac says. "I'm sorry."

"Yeah, it is messed up." I pause, glancing at the cages. "I volunteer here, and Rachel helps sometimes. So I was going to take our favorite dog to visit her. We're not really supposed to do that, but Marnie is pretty awesome."

"Yeah, she seems nice." Ezekiel sits in a cage by Isaac. He wags his tail, and I mouth *soon*.

"What about you?" I ask. "You said you're supposed to be at practice?"

Isaac hesitates. He slips that red stress ball out of his pocket and squeezes it twice. I didn't realize he always carried it around. "I sprained my ankle at the game last night," he says. "If I play on it, I could injure it worse, and I won't be able to play the rest of the season. I'll lose my chance of getting a scholarship." His fingers grip the ball so tight they go white. "But if I *don't* play, scouts won't see me at the upcoming game, and I could lose my chance of getting a scholarship. It's only a sprain—" His voice catches. "—but it could ruin everything."

Something breaks within me.

It shouldn't be like this. It shouldn't be this hard.

Isaac looks like he's on the verge of tears. I wonder if I look much different. "C'mon," I say, unlatching Ezekiel's cage. "We can play with him outside before I take him home."

"Do you have time? With your sister and all…"

"I have time," I say. Ezekiel scrambles into Isaac's arms and licks his face. Isaac laughs and pulls him closer. "I can make time."

Later that afternoon, I knock on Rachel's bedroom door. After she was discharged from the hospital, with a follow-up appointment set with a pediatric psychologist, she came home and napped. So did my parents. It was strange being at home on a Saturday without attending synagogue first. I was too anxious to nap, so I went to the animal shelter instead.

"Come in," Rachel calls.

I open her door. "The Chain" by Fleetwood Mac plays from her iPad. Great music taste definitely runs in the family.

"Someone's here to see you," I say, keeping Ezekiel out of her sight.

"Who?" Rachel asks. "Sara?"

"Nope." I bend down and unhook the leash. Ezekiel races into the room and jumps onto the bed, licking Rachel's face. She squeals and hugs him.

"Oh my god!" she says. "Is he ours?"

"Oh, oops. Unfortunately not." I wince. "Mom is still allergic. But guess what? My friend Isaac and his family are going to adopt him!"

"Really?" Rachel asks, excited.

"Really! And Isaac said we can come over and play with Ezekiel whenever we want."

"Oh good." Rachel grins. Ezekiel tries to climb onto her chest and ends up haphazardly hugging her, one paw stretched out to her neck, another on her stomach. Rachel leans down and cuddles him, breathing deeply. "I love him," she says.

"Me too." I climb on the bed with them and pet Ezekiel, but he only gives my hand a tiny lick and stays curled up against Rachel.

We sit with him for a long time, talking about nothing more serious than his cute puppy tail and his cute puppy face. But then, Rachel says, "I'm scared to go to the psychologist. Have you ever been to one?"

"I haven't," I say. Though maybe it's a good idea to talk to someone. Doing this alone isn't working, so maybe it's time to try something new. "I'm sure she'll be really nice. Besides, Mom and Dad are awesome. They won't make you keep going if you don't like it."

"I looked it up," Rachel says.

"Psychology?"

"Psychosomatic response." She pronounces the words

deliberately, like she's still getting used to them. "It's kind of scary your head can make you sick. How am I supposed to get my homework done if working can hurt me?"

I stay silent, thinking about all the times I told myself skipping sleep was fine, skipping lunch was fine, all to get the work done. "I wish I knew. I wish I could tell you to stop, but I'm not sure how we can stop school. Maybe the psychologist can help."

"Maybe."

How *do* you avoid school stress when you can't avoid school?

Ezekiel crawls over to my lap, resting his head on my thigh. My stomach twists with guilt. How can I tell Rachel school doesn't matter when it does? She has so many years of it ahead of her. What if these classes keep tearing her apart from the inside out? I've never wanted the right answers more.

"I love you, *Ra-chell*," I say.

"Love you too."

"I'm always right here." I bang the wall between our rooms. "You know that, right?"

"I know." She shifts under her covers. "I think I'm gonna nap more. I'm tired. Can Ezekiel stay with me?"

"Sure, I'll take him back later."

Rachel snuggles more deeply into bed. I stand and walk into the hallway, but I leave the door cracked open. That way I can keep an eye on her.

FIFTEEN

Sook avoids eye contact with me as she walks into our English class. On Sunday, she brought over Rachel's favorite chocolate chip oatmeal cookies and made light small talk, but only for my sister's sake. I wanted to know how the gig went but was too nervous to bring it up myself. Did they play without me? Was an agent there? And the question I keep trying to push away: Did I ruin her chance at her dream?

Now it's Friday, and we haven't spoken all week. I've barely spoken to anyone all week, drifting from class to class, turning in work and taking tests, but feeling like I'm watching an avatar of myself go through the motions.

My apologies to Sook sit on our text thread unanswered. I've never messed up like this before. I want to fix it. I need to fix it. But I don't know how.

"Hey," I say.

She puts in headphones and opens her leather planner.

Hey isn't going to cut it.

Things are also strained with Amir. I apologized again at school, and he said it's fine, which historically and universally means it's not fine. But I don't know how to make it right with him, either. I fractured two of the most important relationships in my life, and they both need time and attention to repair.

But I'm *tired*.

Part of me wants to put my head down, finish the school year, and dedicate any spare time to Rachel. She had her first appointment with the psychologist earlier this week, and she said it went well, but she's been quieter than usual.

Mom and Dad went into her school and had a talk with her teachers. They apologized profusely and said they had no idea Rachel was putting so much pressure on herself. They said she could stop working on her pirate project, but that's only one assignment of one class of one grade. Mom and Dad can't run into school every time Rachel has a project. I've heard them talking about putting her in a private school next year, one with a more creative learning structure, but Rachel doesn't want to leave her friends.

She needs me. That's where all my free time should go. But I need my friends back. They're my people. I can't be there for my sister if I'm falling apart.

"Sook—" I start again.

Mrs. Rainer enters the room. "All right, class, time for our morning writing prompt."

Sook turns toward the board, away from me. I sigh, then pull out my notebook and #2 pencil and begin to write.

The front doors of the synagogue are locked. We only keep them unlocked during Shabbat services because there are so many people coming in and out, and an officer guards the parking lot.

I press the buzzer. "Ariel Stone. I have a meeting with the rabbi."

"Afternoon, Ariel." The lock clicks. "Come on in."

I open the door. Someone else is coming up behind me, a delivery woman with a small box. Instinct tells me to keep the door open for her, but the security protocol kicks in. I let the door close and send her a sheepish smile. She smiles back. She gets it. Rabbi Solomon wanted to meet at four, so it made sense to come straight after school. But now I'm early, so I guess I'll wander around for a bit.

The sanctuary sits in the middle of the shul. It has giant wooden doors and stained-glass paneling. A rack of tallit and kippahs sit outside it. I place my hand against the lacquered wood and step closer. Even though the sanctuary is empty, I can close my eyes and hear the chorus of prayer. I breathe in gently, once, twice. Calm washes over me.

Eventually, I step away and trail down the hall, passing photos of synagogue presidents and Hebrew school graduating classes. I spot my seventh-grade photo from my bar mitzvah year. I stand in the second row. Red, chubby cheeks. Khakis already half an inch too short. Isaac sits in front of me, glasses perched on his nose.

I spent four days a week with everyone in that picture. Sunday school, plus after-school classes on Tuesday and Thursday, plus services on Saturday and the bar and bat mitzvah parties to go along with them. We all knew each other well, despite being in different social groups at school. I only talk to a few of them now, mostly the kids in my AP classes like Isaac. My social circle has grown small over the years. And now, the few people I still hang out with aren't talking to me.

My alarm buzzes in my pocket. Time for my meeting. I walk down to Rabbi Solomon's office and knock.

She calls out, "Come in."

As I head inside, it hits me that this is the third time I've been here in a month.

"Have a seat, Ariel. Would you like some tea?"

I almost say no. But it's a Friday afternoon, and I'm relatively caught up on my work. Turns out your friends not speaking to you frees up time. My Harvard interview is tomorrow, but I'm ready for that since I've been preparing since it was scheduled. So, strangely, I have an empty evening ahead of me. "Sure, thanks."

"I have some more mandel bread, too." Rabbi Solomon winks, then flicks on the electric kettle next to her desk.

A few minutes later, we each have a steaming mug of Israeli tea and a hunk of mandel bread. I dip mine into the tea, then take a bite.

"So, Ariel. How did your reading go?"

Earlier in the week, when we made the appointment, she asked me to read a story from the Talmud. It was short, only a page. And it was nice to read something and know that I didn't have to write an essay about it.

"I liked it," I reply.

And I did. We discuss the story. It's called "The Fox in the Vineyard." A fox spies luscious grapes in a vineyard, but the hole in the fence is too small. He can't get through. So he starves himself for three days until he can slip through and gorge on the grapes. But once he's eaten all the grapes, he can't get back through the fence. He must fast for three more days and leaves as unsatisfied as he came.

"How do you interpret the story?" Rabbi Solomon asks.

"Well, my first thought was his eyes are bigger than his stomach, but I think it's more than that. It's like he was chasing something pointless. He starved himself for six days for nothing.

He thought the grapes would make him happy, but in the end, it was a waste of time."

"So it's about fruitless activities?" Rabbi Solomon grins and holds up her hands. "Pun not intended, I promise."

"Ha, yeah, I don't know. It's confusing. How do you know if a goal is worth it until you get it? We work hard for a lot of stuff. Should we not put in effort because the reward might not be what we thought?"

"Those are big questions, Ariel."

"I guess." I scratch my ear. "So do you have any answers?"

"It's not so much about the answers. Answers end a conversation. Questions keep a conversation going. We're here to discuss and explore. Why cut off a journey before we get started?"

"But why ask questions if you're never going to get the answers?"

Rabbi Solomon grins. "See, you're already in the habit. Answer a question with a question. That's rabbinical method."

Rabbi Solomon stirs her tea. "What other questions do you have, Ariel? What's been on your mind?" Her face softens. "I heard about your sister. Would you like to talk about it?"

"I guess it's kind of like the story. Rachel and I both want to do well in school. If you do well, you get into a good college and get a good job and make good money..." I glance down at my hands. "But what if we do all of that, and we're too tired to enjoy the reward?"

"What if you get the grapes but you're too full to appreciate them?"

"Something like that," I say. "But I can't just *stop*. It's school. I can't drop out. How are we supposed to do everything right without burning out?"

Rabbi Solomon's eyes flicker with something—with sadness. "That's a tough question, Ariel."

"Got a Talmud story for it?"

Half an hour later, I leave the office and freeze when I see who's sitting on the couch outside. Rabbi Solomon pokes her head out. "Give me five minutes, Malka. I have to make a quick phone call."

"Sure," Malka says with a slight smile.

It's only been a week since I've seen her, but she seems different. Older? I don't know. That's the weird thing about being friends with someone for so long. One day you look at them and realize they're not the eight-year-old kid you built pillow forts with.

"Hey," I say, my shoulders tense.

Except for a text update about Rachel, we haven't spoken since that phone call before the Dizzy Daisies' gig.

She gives a small nod. "Hi."

I scratch the floor with my shoe. "I shouldn't have ditched

you guys," I say. "Not at the last minute, especially without explaining. It was a jerk move. And I'm sorry."

She's silent for a moment, then pats the couch. "Come on. Sit down."

I take the seat next to her. "I'm *really* sorry," I say, my throat tight. I look down and twist my fingers together.

Her voice softens. "Why'd you do it? What's going on, Ariel? I've been worried about you since Yom Kippur."

I bite the inside of my cheek as lies run through my head. No. The truth is better. I clench my fists, then unfurl my fingers and show them to Malka. "This is why."

"Whoa," she breathes out. My skin is covered in blisters and calluses. There are three Band-Aids on particularly bad spots. It actually looks better, at least compared to last week. I haven't had the drive to keep practicing as much for my solo.

"Dr. Whitmore wasn't happy with my solo performance, so she's having me play it against Pari. And if Pari plays better, I'll lose first chair. I couldn't keep practicing for it and the band. And it's not just that—it's my grades, too. Every time I pull up one, another seems to slip. And if I can't fix it, Harvard won't accept me…" I look down. "I don't know what I'm doing wrong."

"Jesus," she says, eyes on my blisters.

"Malka." I tsk. "We're in a synagogue. Jesus isn't involved."

She snorts, and I grin, and some of the awkwardness between us eases.

"I don't understand, though," Malka says. "Why didn't you tell us?"

"I—" I pause. "I was embarrassed. Ashamed, I guess. I'm supposed to have it all together, but I was falling apart. I figured if I worked hard enough, I could secure first chair and pull my grades back up, and everything would be okay. But then I wasn't sleeping enough, and Yom Kippur…"

Malka inhales. "You really scared me, Ariel. All of this scares me. You're endangering yourself, and you endangered me, too."

I swallow hard. "Shit. I'm sorry." Pressure builds behind my eyes. "I'm never going to do that again. You have to believe me. I'm done pushing like that. Look what it did to Rachel. If she keeps at it, this school stuff could—" I rub my eyes. "I don't want to think about what could happen."

"Hey, it's okay. You're okay." She wraps an arm around my shoulder and leans in. "How can I help?"

"I don't know." I sigh. "I want to not care. I *know* Harvard isn't the only place I can get a good education. There are a lot of great colleges. But I can't stop trying altogether, can I? After all of this?"

"I don't think it's an all-or-nothing situation. What about dropping a class? I'm sure you don't need all those APs to graduate."

"Actually, my guidance counselor mentioned that. But it'd be a withdrawal on my transcript. Ugh." I put my face in my hands. "Maybe I need to think about it. I can't do this to myself. I know that. I can't do this to Rachel."

"We'll figure it out. I promise. You have me, you have the rabbi, you have Sook—" She falters.

"What about you?" I glance at Rabbi Solomon's door. "Why are you here?"

Malka tugs on the sleeve of her shirt. "I come sometimes. I started a few weeks ago because I was struggling with the whole *being an adult in college* thing."

"Wait, what?"

"I was driving back here all the time. While everyone else was out sneaking into bars on weekends, I was back in the suburbs with my high school friends. I felt like a loser, like I was failing college life."

"But you aren't a loser! You're our cool, older friend."

She laughs. "Thanks, Ariel. I like *some* campus stuff. Classes and the Chabad events have been cool, but I also like chilling here. At college, it's like I always have to try and be someone. Here, I'm Malka."

"Is it getting any better?"

"Yeah, I've stopped putting as much pressure on myself to, like, do college right. And Rasha and I have become pretty close. She said she went through some similar stuff when she decided to live at home. Now, she's at peace with it."

I nod. "That's good." I nudge her, tucking my head to her

shoulder for a few seconds. "I'm sorry you were going through that, but I'm glad you're doing better. You could've talked to me about it."

"Yeah, and you could've talked to me about school."

We both grin.

"We'll have to do better," Malka says.

"Agreed." I gnaw the side of my nail. "So, uh, how did the show go?"

Malka gasps. "Holy shit! No one told you, did they?"

"Told me what?"

"Well, no agent showed." Relief floods through me. I didn't ruin their chance after all. God, I'm lucky. "But Clarissa was there and mentioned she's playing in a showcase tomorrow at the Georgia Theater in Athens, and one of the bands canceled at the last minute. She put in a word, and we got the slot! And there might be multiple agents attending. Sook is freaking out. We've been practicing nonstop."

"Dude, that's amazing! That's *everything*." It's a huge moment. A huge moment my best friend didn't tell me about. My heart drops. "I'm so happy for you. Seriously. Y'all will be amazing. Is there... Do you need me to..."

Malka grimaces. "Sook is already writing the violin out of the songs. But you could come watch. She's too stubborn to say it, but I know she misses you."

"I'm not sure about that," I say. "I don't want to distract

her and mess up her chance. Also, my Harvard interview is tomorrow."

"Holy shit."

"Yeah."

Rabbi Solomon peeks her head out. "Malka, I'm ready for you."

"Be right in!"

We both stand, and Malka hugs me. It's one of those long, solid ones that reminds me how great hugs can be.

"Maybe I'll see you after? On Sunday?" Malka asks.

"Yeah, that sounds good."

"Hey, if you can make time, you should join me for one of the Chabad events."

"Sure, I will."

"I hope this all gets easier for you," Malka says.

"Thanks." I twist my fingers together, then smile. "I think it will soon."

SIXTEEN

Starbucks is only a few minutes away from my house. I used to come with Pari and Sook and a few other kids for a study group freshman year, when we did more talking than studying.

The bell rings as I open the door. The place is packed, parents with strollers and preteens holding blended drinks with whipped cream. I scan the room until I spot Hannah.

She looks younger than the picture on her website. She's dressed casually in jeans and a white blouse. Crap. I'm in the suit I wore to synagogue. I had time to change, but I thought I was supposed to dress up for a Harvard interview.

God, I look ridiculous.

I clear my throat and walk toward her. Or wait, should I get a drink first? There's already a white mug on the table in front of her. What if she thinks I'm late, though? Okay, say hello, and then get a drink.

She looks up when I'm a few feet away and smiles. "Ariel?" she asks, pronouncing my name correctly.

She doesn't blink twice at my suit. I shake her hand. She has a solid but easy grip. "Hi, so nice to meet you, Ms. Shultz." I rock back on my heels. "I'm going to grab a drink." Right? It'd be awkward to sit down with no drink. "Can I get you anything?"

"Hannah, please. And I've got mine here." She taps her mug. "Take your time."

I get in the line, shifting awkwardly on my feet. There are four people in front of me. Why do so many people drink coffee on the weekends? I wonder if Hannah is watching me. I slip my phone out of my pocket and pull up the short version of the interview notes I emailed to myself, running over facts about Harvard and Hannah and how much I love playing violin in a band. Ha. If only she knew the band is in Athens right now, getting ready to play a show without me. If only she knew I was a selfish person who put my own goals before my friend's goals. The guilt eats at my unsettled stomach.

The line inches forward. Hannah knows I arrived on time, but I still feel like I'm messing up. I should've been here earlier. Like a half hour early, gotten my drink first, and then I could've waited patiently while she was in line. Another minute passes. Way to make an awesome impression.

My pulse thuds in my ears. I take a breath as I finally reach the front of the line.

"What can I get for you?" the barista asks. "Have you tried our new pumpkin hazelnut mocha latte?"

"Uh, sure. One of those."

"Coming right up!"

I pay, then step to the side and wait for my order. Shaking my head, I try to get back in the zone. Don't throw away the opportunity I'm lucky to have. I get my pumpkin hazelnut mocha latte and walk back to Hannah. "Sorry about that." I place the cup on the table, then inch it forward in case I knock it and it spills everywhere.

"No worries." She smiles and grabs a leather notebook from her purse. It reminds me of Sook's planner, and my chest squeezes. "So," Hannah says. "You mentioned in your email that you volunteer at an animal shelter. That's pretty neat. What drew you to that?"

Easy hours. Mom knows the manager.

I pick up my drink, but it's too hot to sip. "I wanted to give back to the community," I answer, my words sounding painfully rehearsed. "And I like animals. It feels good helping them."

"I adopted my dog from a shelter," Hannah says.

"That's awesome!"

She laughs. "He's totally tearing apart my house, but I love him. You have any pets at home?"

"I don't. My mom is allergic."

"Bummer." Hannah nods. "Maybe you can adopt when you live on your own?"

I smile, thinking of having a dog like Ezekiel around to cuddle. "Maybe."

Hannah looks at her notes again. "I also see you're involved with your synagogue. I'm Jewish, too, if you didn't guess by my name. Is a Jewish community something you're looking for at college?"

"I haven't thought about it much," I say truthfully. "My friend likes the Chabad at her school. Is there a Harvard Chabad?"

"There is! I was a member and loved it." Hannah tells me all about it, from Tuesday-night tacos and Torah to having a place to celebrate the High Holidays. It sounds nice, somewhere in a new environment where I could be totally comfortable.

We keep talking, some of my interview anxiety easing away as Hannah tells me about some of her favorite classes and professors, restaurants I have to check out, and the countless campus organizations and activities. There's even an orchestra nonmajors can join. "And I was on the intramural softball team," she says. "Do you play any sports?"

"Yes," I say. "Well, no. I used to play soccer. But I got kind of busy with classes."

"There's a heavy workload at Harvard, for sure," Hannah says, "But a lot of students find they have more free time than in high school. You should check out the intramural team if you end up there."

Hannah excuses herself to the restroom, and I lean back in my seat, imagining all these possibilities. I've been so focused on getting into Harvard, I haven't given much thought to what life will be like there. Already, I can see myself walking across the beautiful campus to class, attending Tacos and Torah with my fellow Jews, joining an orchestra without the dark cloud of Dr. Whitmore, playing intramural soccer and feeling the adrenaline of slamming a ball down the field.

My grades are back up. I'm doing well now. It's only a few months until graduation. Keep this up and my Harvard dream could be real before I know it.

But Rachel's face flashes through my thoughts. I chew the inside of my cheek and check my phone for messages. I have one from Dad that reads: *Good luck!*

And one from Rachel that says: *You got this!*

And then a couple from Malka:

Sook forgot the flash drive with our drum tracks.

There are agents here.

She's freaking out.

We don't have time to drive back.

Show starts in two hours.

I freeze. That last text was sent five minutes ago.

Here I am, daydreaming about my perfect life at Harvard

when my best friend's dream is on the line. I put Athens into Google maps and route the directions. It'll take ninety minutes to get there. If I leave right now, go straight to Sook's house…

This is it.

Sook's chance to get signed.

My chance to get my best friend back.

Hannah returns and sits down. "Now, let's talk about—"

"I'm so sorry," I cut her off, then stand. I can't believe the words leaving my mouth. "I have to go."

She looks concerned. "Is everything all right?"

"Yes. No. I mean, my best friend needs help. She's okay, but…it's kind of hard to explain. I'm sorry."

"All right." Hannah hesitates. "The interview isn't finished. I really like you, Ariel, but I still have a few questions. We could be done in fifteen minutes. Are you sure you need to leave now?"

I waver. Will fifteen more minutes get me into Harvard?

Does getting in matter if I lose my best friend?

"I'm sure," I say, breathless. "It was really great meeting you. Thank you for telling me so much about Harvard." I pause, again imagining what my life could be like on their campus. "I really do think I'd love it there."

Hannah smiles. "I'm glad to hear that, Ariel."

Then I'm out the door before she can say anything else.

"Ariel, you're doing *what?*" Mom asks from speakerphone. I'm already on I-285 with Sook's flash drive in my car. The Who blasts from the car speakers, Keith Moon hammering me down the highway. I turn the volume down.

"I'm driving up to Athens to bring Sook her flash drive so she can play the most important gig of her life."

"Ariel, *what?*"

"I'm driving—"

"Turn the car around. You aren't allowed to drive to Athens without permission. That's almost two hours away!"

"I know. And that's why I can't turn the car around. I'm running out of time to help her, and look, this is really important, okay? I promise. Epically important. And if you disagree, when I get home, you can ground me for the rest of high school, but I'm not turning the car around."

"Ariel, this is not okay."

"I know. I'm sorry."

Mom sighs. I can hear her thinking, giving up a bit of ground. "No texting and driving. You call me the second you get there. And never pull anything like this again. Got it?"

"Got it," I say. "Thanks, Mom. Love you."

"Wait! What happened with your interview?"

I swallow hard. "It went great."

I'm trying not to think about how I might have thrown away everything. But I think this is more important. No, I know it is.

The phone clicks off. I switch into the left lane and press down on the gas.

"I'll park the car," Amir says.

Amir is here, standing outside my car's passenger window.

I blink. No, it's not road fatigue. He's really here. In Athens. In his Hufflepuff T-shirt. His hair is pushed back, with one errant strand falling into his eye. I've seen him at school, but it's been so long since I've *looked* at him.

"I didn't know you'd be here," I say.

He scratches his stubble. "Yeah, well, Rasha's recording a segment for the podcast and asked if I wanted to road-trip with her."

"Yeah..." I can't stop staring at him and his broad shoulders and his dark eyes and his perfect lips.

"You should probably run in. It's four o'clock."

"Shit, yeah." I jump out of the car, leaving it running. I pulled to the curb right outside the theater in downtown Athens. There are, like, a dozen square blocks of bars and restaurants with college kids everywhere, enjoying the fall weather, running from bar to restaurant and back again. One street is blocked off, and a band plays on an outdoor stage, people swaying to the music, beers in hand.

"Huh. This place is awesome."

"Agreed," Amir says. "UGA has a pretty great premed program, too. It's moving up my list."

"That's cool. So—"

"Ariel, go!"

"Right." I laugh, and he does, too. My pulse skips. I miss us. "I'm going, I'm going," I say, still grinning as I race into the venue.

I buy a ticket, then once inside, I call Malka. She picks up right away. "Where are you?" I ask. "I'm here."

"Baruch Hashem. Walk toward the stage. We'll meet you by the side door."

Will Sook be happy to see me? Does Sook even know she's about to see me?

There's no band on stage at the moment, so people are milling about, and it's easy enough to push through the crowd. I pass a group of girls taking shots in the middle of the afternoon, a couple of guys laughing at something on a phone, and a girl wearing a dress with planets on it, beating drumsticks against her leg.

As I near the stage, Malka and Sook exit through a side door. There's a girl with violet hair next to Sook. I recognize her from the Carousels video Sook made me watch. It's Clarissa. She whispers something into Sook's ear and squeezes her hand before Sook and Malka step my way.

"Holy shit," I say. "Y'all look badass."

Sook's wearing a black dress, ripped at the shoulders, and Malka has on black jeans, Converse, and a black tank.

"Thanks," Malka says.

Sook doesn't respond.

I bite the edge of my nail. "So, Clarissa, is that happening?"

After a long moment, Sook says, "We're friends. But maybe one day…" She's unfocused, jittery. "So do you have it?"

I reach into my pocket, terrified for a moment it somehow fell out, but my fingers land on the small flash drive. "Right here." I hand it over.

About a dozen emotions cross Sook's face at once. Then she leaps forward and hugs me tight. "Thank you, thank you, thank you."

I hug her back and inhale. She smells like Sook, fresh soap and something sweet, like there's honey in her shampoo.

"I'm sorry," I say. "I'm so sorry I bailed at the last minute. Is there any way you'll forgive me?"

"Ariel." She stays close and takes one of my hands. When she locks eyes with me, my throat catches. "Malka told me what's going on with you." She looks down for a moment. "I didn't know. I didn't notice. *I've* been the terrible friend, not you. I pushed you to join the band, pushed you to play more songs, pushed you to rehearse extra for the gig. All while you were so stressed over school. I was too focused on myself to see it."

"It's not your fault." I grip her hands. "I didn't want you to know. I didn't want anyone to know. I was…ashamed. I was struggling so much when everyone else—my parents, my classmates, you—have it all together." I take a short breath. "I don't understand why it's so much harder for me."

"It's hard for all of us, Ariel," Sook says. She twists her lips. "Earlier this week I talked to my parents about college. They said their parents put so much pressure on them to get into a good school, they didn't want me to go through that. They figured with Dartmouth I'd almost definitely get in without too much stress."

"Oh, that makes sense."

She smiles. "Yeah, it's actually awesome of them. Except I went and stressed myself out over the band instead." She throws up her hands and sighs. "But there's nothing to be ashamed about, Ariel. No one has it all together. I bet not even your parents. Can you promise me something? Promise me we'll talk about this stuff going forward."

I nod. "I promise."

Sook touches her forehead to mine and inhales, then steps back. "Love you," she says.

"Love you, too."

Malka sniffs, and I turn to see her wiping her eyes. "Oh, shut up," she says. "Hey, how'd your interview go?"

I open my mouth and close it. I don't need to tell them I left early. Not to lie—I just don't want them feeling bad, or making it seem like I'm some martyr. They deserve this. "It went well, I think. We'll see."

"Yay! Fingers crossed. You going to stay for the show?"

"Yes," a voice behind me says. "He's going to watch with us."

I turn and find Amir with Rasha at his side. He's even smiling at me. I need to fix us before his Hufflepuffness runs out.

Ten minutes later, the lights dim, and Sook and Malka take the stage. I stand near the front with Amir and Rasha, feeling grateful and awake. The concert hall fills more and more. People sway and shout and dance. My friends are real musicians. Their songs are real songs. They're playing a real show, and it's *incredible*.

Tears spring to my eyes, and I feel silly, but I also don't feel silly at all. Amir nudges my shoulder. His hand brushes against mine. I take the temporary forgiveness, grasp his hand, and inhale. Spearmint and basil. My body floods with warmth and relief, and for the first time in a long time, I know I'm exactly where I should be.

"You're in trouble," Rachel sings when I walk through the door a little past eight.

"Way to rub it in, sister." I ruffle her curls. She looks better. More like my Rachel. She's wearing her favorite tie-dye dress, and there's Cheetos dust on her fingers.

After the Dizzy Daisies' show, my friends asked me to stay

and go with them to a Motel/Hotel show, some popular EDM band that got their start in Athens. But I knew my punishment would be worse the longer I put off coming home. As I was leaving, a woman with sleek hair started talking to Sook, and by the look on Sook's face, I'm pretty sure the woman was an agent.

"Ariel Moshe," Dad says from the living room. Uh-oh. Full Hebrew name. I'm in trouble.

I ask Rachel, "Can you wait upstairs?"

"Hmph," she says. "Fine."

Mom and Dad are sitting on the love seat together. Mom is kind of curled into Dad, one leg resting over his lap. I smile. I like how much they still like each other.

"Sit," Mom says.

My smile fades.

I plop on the three-seat couch, feeling like a little kid, swallowed up by its size. My phone buzzes in my pocket. Maybe Sook about the agent? Now is not the time to check. I crack my neck left and then right and take a short breath. "Before you guys say anything," I start. "I'm sorry."

Dad pinches the bridge of his nose. "All right," he says. "Explain first. Why did you go to Athens?"

"Sook forgot her drum tracks, and she needed them to play her show."

"So you left after your Harvard interview and drove to Athens? Just like that? Without permission?" Mom asks.

"Actually, I left before my interview ended."

Mom shakes her head. "I don't understand, Ariel. You've been working so hard to get into Harvard, and now you're risking it all? For what? Why?"

"Because Harvard isn't the most important thing!" I snap, surprising us all. Mom slips her legs off Dad's lap, and they both sit up straight.

"*We* know that," Mom says. "But it seems to be all you focus on."

"If it's not important to you, why do you tell everyone I'm applying there? It's all you guys talk about. Like it's the only worthwhile thing about me." My voice begins to shake. "If I don't get in, that's it. I'll be Ariel, the one who didn't get into Harvard. I'll let everyone down. I'll let *you guys* down. And I might not get in. I really might not, because I'm not perfect. They asked for perfect, and I'm not, and I don't know what else I can—"

"Ariel," Mom says, voice breaking.

I realize all three of us are crying.

Dad leans forward. "Ariel." He pauses and meets my eyes. "*Everything* about you is worthwhile." More tears fall, but with them, tension eases from my body. "People ask where you're applying, so we tell them. That's all. They're interested in you, so we tell them."

"Tatala, we don't care where you go to school. Perfect is

overrated." Mom's eyes shine. "Who would want perfect when they could have you?"

I swallow hard and run a hand through my hair. "But what do I do then?" I ask.

Mom walks over and sits next to me. She hugs me, her face damp against mine. "We'll make a plan. Right, Saul?"

"Yes," Dad says. "We'll figure this out together. Ariel, you've done enough on your own. You've worked hard enough. We've got you now. Okay?"

"Okay." I breathe out. "Okay."

SEVENTEEN

"Here." I hand the slip of pink paper to Ms. Hayes.

It's Monday morning, and I walked straight to her office as soon as I got to school. After a long talk with my parents this weekend, we agreed this was the best move, and now I want it done with. I still want to go to Harvard, even more so after my conversation with Hannah, but it's not worth tearing myself apart over it.

Ms. Hayes looks up, surprised. "You're dropping a course?"

"Spanish lit," I say. "I need your signature."

"Spanish lit…" She types into the computer. "But your grade. You have an A in Spanish." She scans the screen. "You have an A in *all* your classes."

"I know," I say. Even my English grade is back up because Mrs. Rainer entered the extra credit. "But—" My throat is tight.

I push through. "It's too much. Spanish lit takes up hours of my time every week, and it's only an elective. It's putting a strain on my other classes, and on me. I need to drop it."

"Ariel, I'm not trying to fight you. I just want to make sure you're considering the situation. Harvard might see this, not to mention schools you apply to regular decision. Are you absolutely sure?"

"Ms. Hayes." Her gaze snaps up to mine. "I appreciate everything you've done for me, genuinely. But this is my decision, and I'm making the right one. If Harvard sees the withdrawal, well, hopefully the rest of my transcript makes up for it. And if it doesn't, it doesn't. You can't guarantee I'll get in if I keep the class, can you?"

"No, but—"

"Then I'm dropping it," I say.

"You might not be valedictorian."

"I know."

"Pari could—"

"I know. Please sign it."

Her eyes search mine. Then, she chuckles, filling out the form with an amused smile on her lips. "Hey, you're running the show."

The rest of the week rushes by. My Spanish teacher was surprised when I told her I was dropping the course, but she didn't argue.

Now it's Friday afternoon, and I'm talking with Amir and Sook in the hallway before AP Gov.

"She told us to keep in touch," Sook says. The agent didn't sign her, but Sook is still bubbling with enthusiasm. "And she said I have a ton of potential and that college towns are great places to get started because there are a bunch of little venues always looking to book bands."

"So wait, you *do* want to go to Dartmouth now?" I ask.

Sook nods. "Yeah, I think so. I mean, I'm only seventeen, right? I have plenty of time to become a famous musician. I guess I could go and get an Ivy League education first."

Amir raises his eyebrows. "*You guess?*"

Sook laughs. "I swear, I don't know what I was thinking turning down that opportunity. Just being a privileged little shit I guess."

Amir shakes his head and smiles at me. We've been texting all the time, and one night we even had an actual phone call that lasted hours, rambling about everything from our favorite Harry Potter creatures to places we'd want to live if we didn't have to go to college to dead musicians I'd want to play music with.

But things still aren't right between us. We haven't kissed since before his photography show. And it's not just because my parents grounded me after my Athens stunt.

I have something epic planned for tonight, and I hope it'll make things good with us again. Getting everything in order has taken more time than I expected. At least my parents are behind the plan, because I had to ask for an exception to my grounding and to dip into my bar mitzvah fund.

"I've been talking to Clarissa," Sook says. "And I think Malka and I might move to Athens for the summer to play our music and get comfortable on stage. I'll miss playing with her, so we're going to make our last months together count."

"Really? That's awesome," I say as I notice Pari walking down the hallway. She's wearing chunky headphones and a hoodie sweatshirt. On Wednesday, we both played the solo for Dr. Whitmore. I hadn't practiced for days, but it wouldn't have mattered anyways because Pari was masterful. When Dr. Whitmore told me I was dropping to second chair, I felt a twinge of panic, then relief. Pari deserves first chair, and I don't need to bloody my fingers more to fight it.

"I'll see you guys later," I tell Amir and Sook, turning and speed-walking down the hall. "Pari!" I call. She doesn't hear me. I walk faster, until I'm right behind her, and tap her on the shoulder. She spins around, startled. "Crap," I say. "Sorry."

She keeps her headphones on.

"Can we talk?"

It looks like she's going to ignore me, but then she nods and slips off her headphones. We move around a corner, off to one of the short, empty hallways leading to an emergency exit.

"What?" she asks, voice curt.

"I'm sorry." I tug my backpack strap. "I'm sorry about the other day. I was a jerk. This school pressure, it's been a lot for me. I know you're not as affected by it…"

"Ariel. What? I'm as affected as you."

"You are?"

"Of course, I am! I'm a person, Ariel." She shakes her head. "When I found out you were taking that computer science class? It almost broke me. I put in all that work, and I was going to lose my shot at valedictorian because I missed signing up for one class? I don't blame you for signing up and not telling me, but you were so damn elitist about it. Like congratulations, you're *so* smart. You gamed the system better." She takes a breath. "Not to mention, I deal with a lot more shit than you do. You're a guy. It's cool for guys to be successful. But if a girl wants to achieve the same level of success, we're annoying. Like we're asking for too much."

"Oh," I say. "I didn't realize—"

She keeps going. "It took months, but I finally accepted that I didn't have a chance at being number one, and then you tore into me. I was only trying to help you, and you were a jerk." Her gaze meets mine. "I never wanted to be your competition, Ariel. I just wanted to be your friend."

My stomach drops, her words hitting hard. After a long moment, I say, "I'm sorry. Really sorry. I was so focused on myself…I should've never treated you like that."

"No, you shouldn't have." She shifts on her feet. "We're all stressed. This place does that to us."

"It used to be okay. Fun even. Remember freshman year?"

"Yeah, we were all in it together then. It was exciting. And I felt cool, you know? Smart. Capable. But then the workload got ridiculous, and people got intense, and it didn't feel supportive anymore."

"Yeah."

Pari picks at her yellow nail polish. She must sense me watching. "Nervous habit," she says. "Like your neck cracking and nail biting."

My eyes widen. "Wow, call me out."

She grins and puts her hands down. "Sorry. I'm observant."

"Well, maybe we could be in it together again. We have that AP Gov test coming up. Want to study with me?"

Pari gives a soft smile. "Yeah, that sounds nice. Can I bring Isaac?"

"Absolutely. I'll see if Sook can join, too. It'll be a group study hang."

"We probably won't get much work done."

I grin. "I'll get a B if you do."

Pari's smile reaches her eyes. She holds out her hand for a shake. "Deal."

———————————

"I'm here! I'm home!" I shout, closing the front door behind me.

The Naeems are already here for Shabbat dinner, their voices echoing from the kitchen. Amir stands in the entryway.

"Shabbat Shalom," he says.

My cheeks warm. "Shabbat Shalom."

"Where have you been? I didn't see you after class today."

I scratch behind my ear. "Oh, you didn't. I was—"

"Tatala, come here!" Mom calls from the kitchen.

"See you in a second." I hurry away before Amir can press. He didn't see me after class because I had to leave school early to finish getting ready for tonight. It was my first time skipping class. Amir has been so kind, so forgiving, again and again. And I want to show him I know it and I appreciate it.

It was kind of scary, walking out of the school doors, knowing I was missing material. But my parents literally encouraged it. They gave me a fake doctor's appointment note and even said I could skip once a month until graduation if I want. They think it'll be *good* for me.

And it did feel kind of good.

Sook and Malka met me after class. They're still preparing while we're at Shabbat dinner. Things weren't quite ready when I left, but they were almost there. I hope this works. I hope Amir fully comes back to me.

Ten minutes later, we're all settled at the table, except for Mom and Rachel. They say the prayer for the candles. "Baruch atah adonai eloheinu melech haolam asher kideshanu bemitzvotav vetzivanu lehadlik ner shel Shabbat."

As Rachel sits, I lean over and whisper, "We're having a sibling date tomorrow night, okay?"

"What are we doing?"

I grin. "It's surprise."

She narrows her eyes but grins, too. "Hmm, okay."

After this weekend of surprises, I'm planning to sit down and finish my Harvard application on Sunday. Now that I'm officially second chair, there's no reason to wait to hit submit. I've done all that I can, and I'm scared, but I'm ready for the rest to be out of my hands.

The house smells amazing, thanks to the giant pot of matzo ball soup on the stove and the cedar plank salmon Dad made. Everyone's phones sit on the breakfast bar, stacked on top of each other so no one is able to check without us all seeing it. Even though we don't turn off electronics for Shabbat, I love that we go off the grid for at least an hour.

"What a beautiful table," Mrs. Naeem says, using the tongs to fill her plate with spinach salad.

"Gorgeous," Mr. Naeem agrees. "Amir, you should take a picture."

"*Dad*, stop," Rasha says. "Leave him alone about the photography."

Mr. Naeem tsks. "I'm simply saying it's a beautiful table. I understand Amir here is going to be a fine doctor. Right, Amir?"

His eyes shine with pure happiness. "Right, Dad."

As the conversation moves on, I nudge Amir and whisper, "When did that happen?"

"During the disappearance of Ariel Stone." He raises an eyebrow. "I was…frustrated. And I let out that frustration by finally telling my parents to stop pushing photography. And by telling them, I mean, yelling at them. Loudly."

"Very loudly," Rasha chimes in. She kisses his cheek. "You fit right into the family now."

Rasha pops a piece of challah in her mouth, and Sara grabs the rest of her slice. "Hey," she says. "There's enough to go around, you know!"

"Yeah, but I wanted yours!"

Sara giggles and Rachel laughs, too. They're funny that way. One usually can't laugh without the other. Rachel's eyes are bright. While we were preparing dinner, she wouldn't stop talking about a new pirate she discovered. A girl in her class did a presentation on her, and Rachel was so interested that she demanded we go to the bookstore so she could find out more about her. My parents said yes after confirming it was for fun and not an assignment.

They've been watching us both carefully, and they're also trying to make changes. Next week, they're going to petition the school board with a bunch of other parents to try and get back fifth-grade recess. Maybe the next generation of kids will get to stay kids a little longer.

I'm making changes, too. In addition to dropping AP Spanish lit, I promised Rabbi Solomon I'd visit twice a month to chat. It's nice to have someone to talk to, and I'm enjoying the stories in the Talmud. My school stress isn't going to disappear, but I can look for more ways to dial it back.

"Want some challah?" Amir asks.

Sitting next to him at a table with our families feels wonderfully normal. "Yes, please." Amir passes me a slice, fingers brushing against mine. He gives me that half smile I love so much, and I can't bite back my own goofy grin. The table is full of munching and laughter, and a feeling of contentment settles over me.

"So." Mom unties her hair, her curls falling around her shoulders. "Bloopers and highlights. Who's going first?"

"This was the perfect suggestion," Amir says as we walk down the block to Elaine's. I'm all nerves. I want to take his hand, but mine is probably clammy, and he might get suspicious. "I haven't been here for a couple weeks. I miss it."

"Good," I say.

"I'm surprised your parents let you out of your grounding for the night. That was nice of them. The soup was delicious, by the way, but I think the matzo balls could've used more time to soften."

I laugh. "What? Suddenly you're an expert?"

"Look, I now know what heaven tastes like. Also, I hope you don't mind, but I'm coming over for Shabbat dinner every week."

"Only if I can come over whenever your dad cooks chicken karahi."

"Deal," Amir says.

We make it to the gallery doors. My heart tries to beat its way out of my rib cage. I swear I can actually feel it pounding against the bones. Sook was originally going to do a guest spot on a podcast tonight, but she volunteered to finish set up instead. I felt bad about her missing the opportunity, but she squeezed my hand and said, *hey, best friend tops music career*.

"Before we go in," I say, turning to Amir. "I want to apologize again. I know your photography show was important to you, and I'm sorry I missed it. School had me—" I give a short sigh.

Amir takes my hand. "You know, Ariel, you're not the only one stressed about school. I struggle in AP Chem and Bio, and I want to be a *doctor*. I should be passing those courses with flying colors. But I shouldn't have to rethink my entire future because AP classes force us to rush through the material." He sighs. "They make us think the grade is more important than the learning, and that's messed up. We're all overwhelmed. You're not alone."

I think of all my classmates, bent over textbooks, shoulders strained under heavy backpacks, eyes hooded from lack of sleep. We're all in it together, whether we want to be or not.

I step forward and kiss Amir's cheek, hesitant about the

show of affection in our mending relationship. But he smiles and squeezes my hand. "C'mon. Let's go in."

We pull open the gallery doors. At first, everything looks normal. There are photographs on the walls. Music plays from the speakers. People in skinny jeans and glasses drink wine and beer.

"Where should we start?" Amir asks.

"Hmm." I hope my voice sounds level. "Maybe the spotlight corner? I loved that artist last time."

"All right." We walk toward the back of the gallery, and when we're close enough to see the photos, Amir freezes. "Ariel, what's going on?"

I turn to him, heart pounding. "I know how much Elaine's means to you," I say. "And I know how much *you* mean to me. And I wanted to make sure you knew it, too."

"Ariel…" His eyes are wide as he stares at the wall of photos.

"C'mon," I say. "Let's look."

We step closer. On the wall, in black decal lettering is his name: AMIR NAEEM. It took a lot to make this happen, but thankfully Amir is well-loved. The owner, Elaine, said she'd be honored to showcase his work.

There's my favorite, the photo of his parents laughing in the kitchen. There's a photo of Sara and Rachel, their hands clasped as they meet Disney's Jasmine at a birthday party, joy in their eyes.

And I've added something special. On the walls, there are

cursive decals with quotes from Harry Potter books. Earlier this week, I was freaking out they wouldn't print in time, but it all came together.

Next to a picture of Sara playing piano, sun streaming in through the window, it says: "Ah, music… A magic beyond all we do here!"

Amir turns to me. "Isn't that from *Sorcerer's Stone*?"

I smile. "Yes."

There's a photo of Rasha, microphone in front of her, with a look so serene it's startling. The quote next to it reads: "Words are, in my not-so-humble opinion, our most inexhaustible source of magic."

Amir turns to me, eyes shining. "Ariel, I can't…how…my work is in Elaine's." His grin is so big, it breaks my heart open. He rubs a hand against his neck. "How did you do this? Why did you do this?"

"Well, I had a little help." I nod behind us, and Amir turns to find Sook and Malka waving. There are other friends here, too—Pari and Isaac and Amir's older friends from their art scene.

"As for why," I say, Amir turning back to me. "It's because I'm so truly, deeply sorry that I missed your show. You've been so forgiving. So amazing. More than I deserve. And I needed to show you how much I care."

He shakes his head slowly. "You must care a lot. I can't

believe I have an exhibit in Elaine's. I have an exhibit in Elaine's, and it's Harry Potter–themed."

I grin. "Oh, that reminds me!" I pull an envelope from my back pocket and pass it to him.

"There's more?" he asks. "What is it?"

"Open it!"

He does, and his eyes widen in excitement. Two tickets to the Atlanta Symphony Orchestra's presentation of *Harry Potter and the Sorcerer's Stone*. "They're going to play the score while showing the first movie," I say.

"This is going to be the most epic thing ever!"

"Really? You're excited? I wanted to get us tickets to Harry Potter World, but my parents weren't thrilled at the idea of us having an overnight together."

Amir laughs. "I don't think mine would've been okay with that, either. Though, maybe after graduation we could…"

My stomach flips. He's thinking of a *we* after graduation.

"Ariel, you're the best boyfriend in the world."

"Boyfriend?" I ask.

"Will you be the Harry to my Cedric?"

"Okay, but they never actually—"

"Shh!" Amir says. "Will you?"

I smile and take his hand, our fingers threading together. His skin is warm and his eyes are warmer.

"I will," I say.

"I know I've said it before, but Ariel—" He takes a deep breath, looking solemn. "I'm really glad you're bad at calculus."

I snort, and Amir laughs, too. "You're the worst," I say.

He grins and steps forward. Our feet bump together, then our chests. My heart skips. "You're the best," he says.

And then he kisses me.

"What are we doing?" Rachel asks again. It's Saturday night. We just picked up frozen yogurt to go and are pulling up to the church's soccer field. The JCC field is locked down at night, but this one is closer to home anyways, and a giant floodlight keeps the dark away.

"*Ariel...*" Rachel says, sliding out of the car. "Tell me!"

"Hold these?" I pass her the yogurts, then open the trunk and grab a soccer ball and worn beach towel. The tacky grip of the ball makes my pulse skip. It's been months since I've laced up cleats and played. I take a quick breath, a smile drawing to my lips, then tell Rachel, "Okay, c'mon."

We walk in silence to the center of the field. It's quiet. The night is so still I can hear the grass fold under our feet. We sit on the towel and look up at the dark sky, a smattering of stars dappling the inky black. Rachel passes me a spoon and my yogurt. There are sour gummy bears on mine. "Cheers," I say.

"Ariel." Rachel dips her spoon into her cup. "Why are we at a church soccer field?"

"To have *fun*."

"Fun?"

"Well, at least I'm going to have fun. When I beat your butt in soccer after finishing this yogurt."

Rachel giggles. "You can't beat me!"

"Oh, yes, I can."

There's a competitive glint in her eyes. She eats her yogurt faster, as if suddenly ravenous. My phone buzzes, and I check it. A text from Amir: *Last night was magical. Thank you.*

We stayed at the gallery until midnight, a dozen of us sitting in a circle on the floor, shoes kicked off, talking about photography and art and life. Amir's hand stayed clasped in mine the entire time. I can still feel the trace of his touch. My cheeks warm, as I think about seeing him tomorrow. And the next day and the next.

"I'm a better player," Rachel says, drawing my attention back to her.

I raise my eyebrows and put my phone away. "You sure about that?"

We finish eating, taunting each other the entire time. Then we get up and kick the ball around, playing on half the field, blocking each other and dribbling the ball toward the net. Rachel cheers as she sinks a goal soundly into the corner. Her curls bounce as she makes her victory lap, both arms pumped in the air, a giant smile on her face.

And I see it, then, a glimpse of what our lives could be.

Rachel passes me the ball, and I run forward.

Dear Reader,

As you now know from reading *You Asked for Perfect*, Ariel and I are big fans of matzo ball soup. After all, it is the best food in the world. And I realized it was wrong to talk about its deliciousness so often without sharing a recipe. So, I present to you my nana's (great-grandmother's) matzo ball soup.

This is the first time my family is writing down the recipe. It's possible this recipe came from generations before my nana. We don't use exact measurements. It's a Schütteherein, which is a Yiddish word to mean it's cooked without a recipe, a pinch of this and a bissel of that, so don't take any measurement too strictly.

I hope you all will enjoy this soup as much as my family has for generations.

Love,
Laura

Yetta "Recht" Eisenman's Matzo Ball Soup

Makes 12 servings

For the Soup

- 2 pounds bone-in kosher chicken*
- 1 large yellow onion
- 7½ quarts water
- 6 to 9 Telma chicken stock cubes (to taste)
- 3 to 4 large carrots
- 3 to 4 large celery stalks
- ½ ounce dill
- Bissel of pepper

Peel half the skin off the chicken (so it isn't too greasy). Peel the onion, but keep the onion whole.

Bring the water, Telma cubes, chicken, and onion to a boil in large saucepan, then cook for 90 minutes on medium heat.

Peel the carrots, then chop the carrots (not too small!). Slice the celery stalks lengthwise and then chop each piece about ⅓ inch long.

Remove the chicken from the pot to cool.

Add carrots, celery, dill, and pepper to the pot and continue cooking on low to medium heat.

After the chicken has cooled enough, pull it off the bone, then put the chicken sans bones back into the pot.

Taste after about an hour; and add more Telma cubes, dill, and pepper if needed. Cook for another hour, then remove from heat to let soup cool in the pot. Once it's cooled, place it in the fridge to store overnight.

In the morning, take the pot out of the fridge and skim off the dill and about 70 percent of the schmaltz (the chicken fat that has risen to the top of the soup). Then heat on low.

For the Matzo Balls**

- 6 eggs
- 6 tablespoons vegetable oil or melted schmaltz
- 1½ cups matzo meal
- 6 to 8 quarts water
- 2 teaspoons baking powder
- ½ teaspoon salt
- ½ teaspoon pepper

In a large mixing bowl, beat the eggs (this helps make the matzo balls fluffier***). Then, blend beaten eggs with vegetable oil or schmaltz.

Add matzo meal and stir with a fork until evenly mixed. Chill mixture in fridge for about 20 minutes.

In the meantime, pour 6 to 8 quarts water into a pot and bring to a brisk boil.

Remove chilled mix from the fridge, then wet your hands and form the matzo balls, each one about 1 inch round. Mixture should make 18 to 24 matzo balls.

Drop the matzo balls into the boiling water and then cover the pot tightly. Reduce heat to a simmer and cook for about 40 minutes. Drain and add the matzo balls to the soup to finish cooking.

The soup is ready when the house smells like chicken soup! If you're looking for a number, it should be ready about an hour after you add the matzo balls so they have time to absorb the flavor, but the soup can simmer for hours after that.

*Must use kosher chicken. It has an extra bit of salt flavor that makes all the difference.

**It is acceptable to use matzo ball mix by Manischewitz or Streit's if you don't wish to make it from scratch. Just add ½ teaspoon baking powder to make the balls fluffier. No more, or they'll fall apart.

***If you need help making your matzo balls even fluffier, also add a tablespoon of seltzer water when making the matzo meal mixture.

ACKNOWLEDGMENTS

Mom and Dad, this book wouldn't exist without you. Not only because you gave birth to me but also because of your constant love and support. We were all dealt some really tough hands, but we keep getting through it together. Thank you for always being there for me. And Dad, thank you for all of the dog pictures. And Mom, thank you for all of the matzo ball soup. I love you both so much!

Elise LaPlante, thank you for being my person. I have the best best friend in the world, and everyone is jealous. I love you forever and know there are so many bright things in your future.

Bubbie and Papa Bobby, thank you for being loving grandparents. I'm so lucky to still have you both in my life. Lauren Sandler Rose and Melissa Sandler, thank you for being such wonderful cousins. I know I can depend on you both, and I'm so grateful for it. Thank you to all of my loving aunts and uncles and cousins.

Katie King and Abbie Blizzard, college was just okay until I found y'all. Thank you for all the bar hopping and game nights and weekend trips. I love you both and hope we're together again soon.

Anna Meriano, Amanda Saulsberry, and Kiki Chatzopoulou, graduate school brought us together, but it couldn't break us apart. Over three years later, and we still talk almost every day. Y'all bring me so much comfort and joy, and I don't know how I would've gotten through the last few years without you. I'm so proud to have you as my friends. Words and Thai will never die. I love you all.

Lauren Vassallo, yes, you get your own paragraph, because you are the best damn critique partner a girl could ask for and an incredible friend on top of that. Could I write books without you? Maybe, but they definitely wouldn't be as good. Thank you for reading so many pages and always providing me with the best insights and advice. I hope 2019 brings you all the happiness!

Jim McCarthy, thank you for being the absolute best agent. I'm more and more grateful each year to have you by my side. Your support and guidance mean so much to me. I don't know how I would navigate publishing without you, but thankfully, I don't have to.

Sourcebooks, you are such a kind and supportive publisher.

Thank you to my editor, Annette Pollert-Morgan, and thank you to my friend Stefani Sloma. And thank you to the entire team, including but definitely not limited to: Steve Geck, Cassie Gutman, Sarah Kasman, Katy Lynch, Beth Oleniczak, and Kate Prosswimmer.

Thank you to all of my friends, critique partners, sensitivity readers, and people who answered questions to help me write this book. I'm so very grateful for you all: Samira Ahmed, Becky Albertalli, Rachael Allen, Jonathan Goldhirsch, Deborah Kim, Elie Lichtschein, Katie Locke, Katherine Menezes, Christy Michell, Ameema Saeed, Evan Sniderman, Jenny Snoddy, Angie Thomas, Kayla Whaley, and Jason Wien.

Thank you to all of the incredible readers, booksellers, librarians, and teachers out there. This book is very near and dear to my heart, and I'm unspeakably grateful for everyone who reads and supports it.

To those readers in school right now—your grades do not define you. I love you.

Thank you and apologies in advance to anyone who I forgot to list. I'm incredibly lucky to have so many wonderful friends in my life. Thank you all for supporting my dreams and me.

Love,

Laura

ABOUT THE AUTHOR

Laura Silverman received her MFA in writing for children from the New School. She loves books, dogs, and sour candy. She currently lives in Atlanta, Georgia. You can say hello on Twitter @LJSilverman1.

DON'T MISS
GIRL out of WATER

Sometimes leaving home is the only way to find yourself

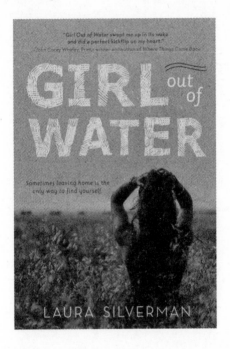

"*Girl Out of Water* swept me up in its wake
and did a perfect kickflip on my heart."

—John Corey Whaley, Printz winner and
author of *Where Things Come Back*

FIREreads

#getbooklit

Your hub for the hottest young adult books!

Visit us online and sign up for our
newsletter at FIREreads.com

 @sourcebooksfire

 sourcebooksfire

 firereads.tumblr.com